COOPER'S CORNER CHRONICLE

Twin Oaks Celebrates First Anniversary

It's been one year since Maureen Cooper and her brother, Clint, opened their doors to welcome guests to Twin Oaks Bed and Breakfast.

"Running a B and B is a dream come true," says Maureen. "It's hard work, but the rewards make it worth it." After living in New York City for so many years, both Clint and Maureen have been delighted—and surprised—at how well their families have adjusted to life in a small town. "The kids are thriving here," says Maureen.

Although no festivities are planned to mark the anniversary, Maureen points out that the past year has truly been one unending celebration. At last count, the romantic atmosphere of Twin Oaks was responsible for eleven weddings, with many former guests returning to the century-old farmhouse to celebrate their big day. The magic of the B and B has even touched the owners themselves. Clint Cooper is currently on honeymoon with his new wife, Beth Young, the town librarian and Twin Oaks pianist.

When asked if she'd like a little magic in her own life, Maureen just laughs. "Been there. Done that! The romantic part of *my* life is over! I'll just enjoy all the wonderful romances around me, and be glad that Twin Oaks helped make them happen."

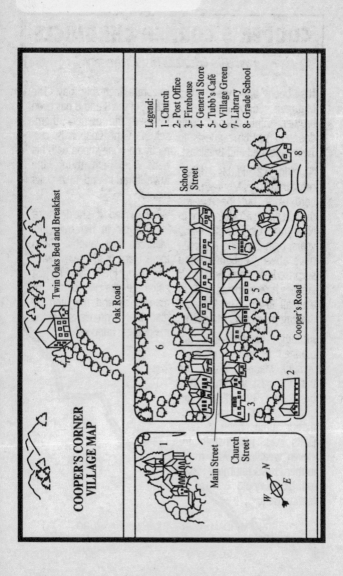

COOPER'S CORNER
VILLAGE MAP

Twin Oaks Bed and Breakfast

Oak Road

Main Street

Church
Street

Cooper's Road

School
Street

Legend:
1- Church
2- Post Office
3- Firehouse
4- General Store
5- Tubb's Café
6- Village Green
7- Library
8- Grade School

W — N — E

COOPER'S CORNER

BOBBY HUTCHINSON

Far from Over

HARLEQUIN®

TORONTO • NEW YORK • LONDON
AMSTERDAM • PARIS • SYDNEY • HAMBURG
STOCKHOLM • ATHENS • TOKYO • MILAN • MADRID
PRAGUE • WARSAW • BUDAPEST • AUCKLAND

For Marsha Zinberg, who's been there for me since the beginning. Your friendship, generosity, humor and editorial expertise are much appreciated.

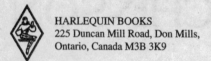

HARLEQUIN BOOKS
225 Duncan Mill Road, Don Mills,
Ontario, Canada M3B 3K9

ISBN 0-373-61263-X

FAR FROM OVER

Bobby Hutchinson is acknowledged as the author of this work.

Copyright © 2002 by Harlequin Books S.A.

Visit us at www.eHarlequin.com

Printed in U.S.A.

Dear Reader,

Writing continuity was a new experience for me, one that I've enjoyed immensely. It was exciting and rewarding to work more closely than usual with both editors and other writers.

Writing forces the exploration of one's deepest emotions. This particular book brought back one of the fears every parent harbors, that of having a beloved child disappear. One of my three sons was deaf, and he also was a master at getting out of locked gates. More times than I care to remember, I called the Vancouver police, panicked because David had wandered away and I couldn't find him. Calling him wasn't an option—he couldn't hear me. With the help of God and Vancouver's finest, I always located him. He's an adult now, with daughters of his own, but those terrified hours I spent riding around in a police car searching for him came back to me in vivid, gut-wrenching detail as I wrote about Maureen. Writing this story was cathartic for me. I hope reading it is a pleasure for you.

Love always,

Bobby Hutchinson

THE COOPERS OF COOPER'S CORNER

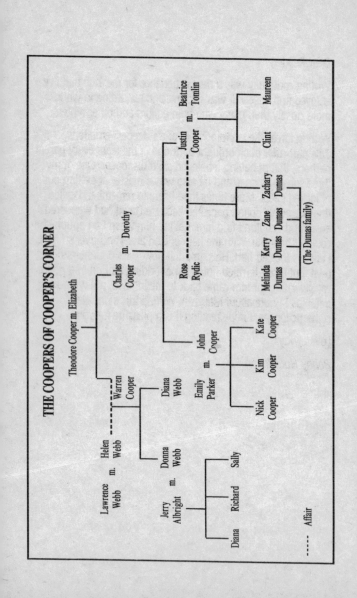

Theodore Cooper m. Elizabeth

Lawrence Webb m. Helen Webb

Warren Cooper

Charles Cooper m. Dorothy

Justin Cooper m. Beatrice Tomlin

Donna Webb

Diana Webb

Rose Rydic

Clint

Maureen

Jerry Albright m. Donna Webb

Emily Parker m. John Cooper

Melinda Dumas

Kerry Dumas

Zane Dumas

Zachary Dumas

Diana

Richard

Sally

Nick Cooper

Kim Cooper

Kate Cooper

(The Dumas family)

----- Affair

CHAPTER ONE

"MOMMY, CAN I PULL THIS ONE?"

Four-year-old Randi Cooper squatted on her plump haunches and closed her fingers around a handful of Queen Anne's lace, ready to tug it out of the soil.

"Nope, punkin. That's a flower."

Maureen looked around and then gestured at a weed.

"Here, my big helper, pull this one out instead."

Randi closed both fists around it and gave a determined heave. The weed burst out of the ground, showering Randi and her twin sister, Robin, with soil. Randi lost her balance and fell backward, spread-eagled, landing in the bed of black-eyed Susans. She lay on her back, squinting blue-green eyes against the warmth and intensity of the early September sun, giggling up at her sister and mother.

"Look at me," she crowed. "I fell down and got all—"

"Dirty," her twin sister supplied. "You got dirty. Get up, Randi." Robin scowled at her twin and did her best to haul her to her feet. "You're smashing all of Mommy's flowers."

"It's okay, they'll grow again." Laughing, Maureen

dusted off the girls' blue shorts and matching shirts, admiring the way the sun picked out rich red high-lights in their thick mass of curling chestnut hair. She gave each a smacking kiss on tanned, satiny cheeks, her heart swelling with love for her beautiful little daughters.

"Gardening with you guys is definitely an adventure. Let's go pick some tomatoes. We can have them in sandwiches for lunch." The kitchen garden was overflowing with autumn's bounty, just as the wild-flower seeds she'd planted so haphazardly last spring had turned into this glorious and amazing array of bee balm, black-eyed Susans, clematis and sunflowers.

It was Maureen's first attempt at gardening, and the results amazed and delighted her. Her brother, Clint, had warned her several times, his eyes twinkling, that she was never going to impress an eligible suitor if all she talked about was the size and abundance of her tomatoes and zucchinis.

Maureen smiled good-naturedly whenever Clint talked about suitors, but the truth was, there was a sore place in her heart when it came to men. She'd decided that marriage wasn't something she'd try again any-time soon, and as for romance—she was far too busy with the twins and the bed-and-breakfast she and Clint ran to even think about it.

Most of the time.

"Let's go pick tomatoes," Randi reminded her, tug-ging at her hand, and Maureen led the way to the vegetable plot. Its relatively small area overflowed with beets, carrots, immense and colorful summer squash, snap beans and four huge pumpkins, the twins' pride and joy.

Maureen had promised the girls that she and Clint, helped by Clint's son, Keegan, would carve the pumpkins into amazing jack-o-lanterns, come Halloween.

The rich soil here in the Berkshires allowed even a novice to produce a quantity of produce that would feed several families well for months. Maureen often wished she could give some of her lavish autumn bounty to old friends in New York, but she didn't go to the city anymore, even though she'd lived there for years. In so many ways, it wasn't a safe or healthy place for either her or her twins.

With the girls' enthusiastic assistance, she picked three fat tomatoes and a handful of fresh basil, remembering that the extent of her gardening in New York had been limited by the size of her tiny balcony.

Moving here to Cooper's Corner, the small, sleepy village in the Berkshire Hills of Massachusetts where she had spent the early years of her childhood, had been good for her and her babies, she mused, grinning as the twins plucked yet another fat, ripe tomato and then shared bites from it, dribbling warm red juice down their chins and making appreciative noises.

"As usual, you guys are gonna need a bath before lunch."

Maureen savored the sunshine on her bare legs, the rich odors of loam and green things growing all around her, the sound of her daughters chattering to each other. This morning, life was good.

She'd had her share of problems since she'd made

the move, but a morning like this reinforced her conviction that this was the place she was meant to raise her girls and live out the rest of her life.

"Aunt Maureen?" The kitchen door of the old farmhouse burst open and another tousled chestnut head appeared.

"Some people just came," Maureen's thirteen-year-old nephew, Keegan, announced. "Some *guests* just arrived," he corrected with a grin that revealed straight white teeth still too large for his adolescent features. It was Friday, a professional development day for teachers, so Keegan was home from school.

"See, Aunt Maureen? I remembered this time." He gave her a cheeky salute and she laughed. She'd corrected him numerous times, insisting that he use the proper terminology for the guests who came to stay at the Twin Oaks B and B.

As well as his shining head of dark reddish-brown hair, Keegan had Maureen's and Clint's jade-green eyes, and his gangly frame already indicated that he'd be tall like the Coopers. Clint was six three, and Maureen, at five eleven, still endured comments from her brother about being the shrimp in the family.

The dramatic line of Keegan's square jaw and the distinctive shape of his ears, however, came from his mother, Kristin. Maureen felt a twinge of sorrow even now when she thought of Kristin Cooper.

Clint's beautiful young wife had died suddenly almost three years ago, but Clint had recently found a new love. He and Beth Young, the local librarian from Cooper's Corner, were married a week ago, right here at Twin Oaks, and were away having fun on their honeymoon. Maureen was thrilled for her brother.

"I took the *guests* into the living room and told them I'd come and get you," Keegan reported.

"You are such a fantastic butler," Maureen teased, grinning at the way Keegan rolled his eyes. She rubbed at her bare knees, making a halfhearted effort at dislodging the dirt and grass embedded there, then gave a quick brush to the seat of her shorts and gave up. Guests at the Twin Oaks B and B just had to get used to a hostess wearing stained denim shorts and a generous helping of soil on her knees.

As she made her way up the deck stairs and into the newly renovated kitchen, she mused that she certainly preferred good, honest, earthy dirt to the nasty human sort she'd dealt with on a daily basis during her years as a New York police detective. And she'd choose denim shorts and a casual T-shirt any day over the jacket that disguised the .38 special she'd carried in a shoulder holster all those years.

She quickly washed the grime off her hands at the sink and glanced up at the antique wall clock she'd found at an auction. It was nine forty-five. The Joyces were early, but there were no other guests at Twin Oaks at the moment, so their room was ready.

"Keegan, be a sport and keep a close eye on those rascals for me, okay?" Force of habit made her go to the door and carefully scan the back yard. Although it was open all around, Twin Oaks was set on a hill with rolling countryside behind it. No one could approach the house without being seen. She knew she was being overcautious, but Maureen didn't like having the twins out of her sight.

Her policing days might be over, but the instincts she'd developed during her years as a detective were alive and well. There'd been too many unexplained and dangerous incidents in the past months to allow her ever to fully relax.

"Sure thing, Aunt Maureen." Keegan headed out, calling to his cousins.

"Kee-gan, Kee-gan." Both small girls came racing over to their adored older cousin, tugging at his hands.

"Let's play hide-and-seek, Keegan."

"Not *again*." With a martyred sigh that Maureen knew was phony, Keegan agreed. He doted on Randi and Robin, and was always agreeable to a game.

Maureen heard him call, "Okay, I'm it. I'll count to fifty. You two better make fast tracks."

The sound of her daughters' excited squeals and giggles as they galloped off to find a place to hide made her smile as she hurried through the kitchen and down the hall to greet the guests.

Maureen thought again, as she did so often these days, how comforting it was to have her brother, Clint, and her nephew living here at Twin Oaks with her. Being a single parent wasn't easy, and having family around was a blessing. The move from the city had been good for Keegan as well as her daughters.

And now there'd be a new aunt for the twins to pester, once Clint was back from his honeymoon with Beth. The more family the better, Maureen thought, smiling a welcome at the tall, thin couple perched side by side on one of the overstuffed sofas in the gigantic living room. The Joyces looked a bit like storks, and they were dressed in matching khaki pants and white cotton shirts, with identical blue trainers on their feet.

What was it that made long-married couples begin to resemble each other? Maureen wondered. Would it have happened to her and Chance if—

"Harry and Lydia Joyce? Welcome to Twin Oaks." Maureen accompanied the greeting with a wide smile and a firm handshake for each of them. "I'm Maureen Cooper. We'll take care of the registration and then I'll take you up to your room. But first, would you like a glass of apple cider? One of our neighbors makes it from his own apples."

"Why, how nice. We'd love some, thank you." Lydia Joyce had a lovely, melodious voice.

Maureen went into the kitchen, found the jug of cider in the new oversize refrigerator and brought a tray with tall, iced glasses.

Harry and Lydia thoroughly enjoyed the cider. They wanted to know what kind of apples it had been made from, what the pressing process was, and whether or not any preservatives had been used.

Patiently Maureen answered their questions, and for the next half hour she went through the familiar business of checking her guests in and making certain they felt welcomed, pampered and very much at home. She didn't rush the process. That was another of the perks of running her own business.

Her time was her own, to spend as she chose. And she'd chosen, with Clint away, to accept only single bookings, even though it was leaf-peeper season. When he returned, the B and B would be filled to the rafters, but for now, the Joyces were the only guests.

"TIME OUT." KEEGAN MADE the hand sign that he'd taught the twins. Red-faced and breathless from running, the two girls threw themselves down on the grass.

"It's too hot, Keegan," Randi declared. "I'm sweating."

"Can we have some juice?" Robin asked hopefully.

"And cookies." The girl's big treat each day was one of the giant chocolate chip cookies Keegan's dad made. He'd left a big jar of them on the kitchen counter before he left, promising the twins that by the time they were gone, he and Beth would be back.

"I'm going inside to the bathroom, and then I'll bring us a drink," Keegan told the girls, making his way into the house. "You guys find somewhere good to hide and stay there till I look for you, okay?"

They chorused agreement, and he went inside, peeking at them through the window. He knew exactly where they'd go, and grinned as he saw them hightail it to the old wooden shed at the far side of the garden. His aunt used it for tools, and the door was standing open. Just a week before, she'd put an automatic lock on the outside. He watched as the twins went inside and slammed the door behind them.

He raced for the bathroom. He didn't want to be too long, in case they tried to get out and got scared, but at least he knew they were safe for a couple of minutes.

Ten minutes later he came out, balancing juice boxes for them and a soda for himself on a tin tray. He had the key to the garden shed in his pocket, and he'd raided the cookie jar. He dumped everything on the last of the steps leading up to the deck. Nearby was a small wooden table set with toy cups and saucers from the twins' tea party earlier that morning. Matching brown teddies sat patiently waiting for Robin and Randi to come back and play.

"Now, where did those girlies go?" Keegan crooned in a loud voice. "I guess I'll just have to eat all these cookies myself. Yum, yum, yum."

He waited a moment, knowing from past experience that the twins would start hollering from inside the shed at the slightest mention of cookies. Maureen was strict about their diet, and the cookies were a special treat.

Maybe they didn't hear him, he decided, when several moments went by with no sign of either of them.

"Randi? Robin?" He made his way toward the shed. "Where are you, you rascals?"

Keegan ambled through the garden, grinning.

"Are they hiding in these sunflowers? Nope. I'll bet they're in the toolshed—"

He came to an abrupt halt at the door of the shed, unable to take in what his eyes were seeing. His mouth went dry and his heart suddenly began to hammer against his ribs. *It couldn't be. It wasn't possible—*

The heavy wooden door was wide open. The sturdy lock Maureen had installed was lying on the ground.

It had been cut through.

He stepped inside.

"Randi? Robin?" His frantic voice rebounded inside the small, hot space. The wheelbarrow, the spades, the rake—all the gardening tools were there, but the twins were gone.

CHAPTER TWO

KEEGAN FELT STUNNED, unable to move or speak for a long moment. His heart started to pound like a hammer against his ribs, and he stumbled back outside, shading his eyes with a trembling hand, looking up at the surrounding steep hills blazing with the scarlet and gold of autumn. He watched for the slightest movement.

Nothing. No one.

His heart slammed against his chest and his breath wouldn't reach down where it was supposed to go.

"Randi," he called at the top of his lungs, his voice increasingly frantic. *"Randi, Robin, where are you?"*

But there was no answer. There was nothing in sight except an old mangy gray cat picking its way down the path. It bolted at the sound of Keegan's voice.

"Oh, please," he moaned. "Help me to find them. Please, God, help me find them."

He hollered again, his voice breaking, but the twins were gone.

And with that realization, Keegan also knew beyond a doubt that it was his fault.

Terror surged through him, and for a moment he couldn't get his breath and grew dizzy. The twins were gone, and his dad had left him in charge of them and his aunt Maureen. Before he set off on his honeymoon, his dad had said, *Take care of everyone for me while I'm gone, son. You're the man of the house now.*

But instead of taking care of them, he'd lost his little cousins. For one instant, Keegan wanted to run somewhere and hide, disappear until this nightmare was over. Instead, he tore through the back garden and up the stairs, shouting at the top of his lungs for his aunt Maureen.

MAUREEN WAS UPSTAIRS, SHOWING the Joyces their bedroom and bath. She'd put them in the blue room, so called for the lavender flowered chintz spread and ruffled curtains she'd sewn for the spacious dormer bedroom.

"Isn't this just the sweetest room, Harry?" Lydia Joyce was delighted. She smoothed a narrow, much beringed hand over the spread.

Harry was admiring the fireplace and the view of the village. Twin Oaks was set on a hillside, overlooking Cooper's Corner, and the blue room was perfectly situated to get a great view of the little town with its distinctive church steeple and quaint shops.

"Aunt Maureen, come quick!"

The panic in Keegan's voice sent a bolt of terror through Maureen.

She didn't remember pounding down the winding staircase. She didn't realize the Joyces were right behind her. She only knew, the moment she saw Keegan's face, that something horrible had happened.

"What?" Maureen was panting, more from dread than exertion.

"The t-twins," Keegan stammered, green eyes huge and filled with utter terror. "They're gone. I had to go to the bathroom. I saw them go into the shed and the door closed behind them. I knew they were locked in, but when I came out, they were gone. The lock's been cut off—"

Without a word Maureen pelted past him into the yard. In one quick glance, she saw the open gate and raced toward it, shouting the girls' names at the top of her voice, trying to quell the abject fear that clutched at her gut and tightened around her throat.

One glance up and down the lane convinced her the twins weren't there. She saw the lock, and years of training kept her from touching it. There might be fingerprints. She fell to her knees in the dirt, examining the soil for any sign of footprints.

She was unaware of the Joyces, watching helplessly as she ran from the shed to the driveway, desperately calling her daughters, looking for a vehicle, for any sign that might give her some clue. There was none. It would be impossible for a car to come up to Twin Oaks and leave without anyone noticing. The driveway started at the main road, led up to the house, then headed back down in a U shape.

Fighting against the instinctive conviction that the search was futile, she returned to the yard.

Her babies were gone. She wanted to scream, to throw herself down in the dirt and give way to hysterics.

Heaven help her, her darling babies were gone.
Someone had taken them, there was no other explanation. It was Keegan who located the bolt cutters, tossed into the tall grass just yards from the shed.

"Look." He bent to pick them up, and Maureen grabbed his arm, restraining him.

"Don't touch them." Her voice was harsh. "Go in the house and get a plastic bag." Even now, as she fought hysteria, Maureen's training as a police officer surfaced. "There might be fingerprints, both on those and on the lock."

She was peripherally aware now of the Joyces, holding hands and looking at her with wide eyes.

Keegan hurried off to find a bag, and Maureen quickly searched the yard, forcing herself to notice every tiny detail, inch by inch. But there was nothing else except for the remains of a tea party the girls had had that morning on their little table and chairs, and the remnants of the half-eaten red tomato they'd so enjoyed just a short time ago. Maureen picked it up. It still had their teeth marks, and she had to force back the tears that threatened as she remembered the juice trickling down their chins, the sounds of delight they'd made as they greedily devoured the fruit.

Inconceivable as it seemed, she had to accept that there was every possibility her daughters had been kidnapped. The unthinkable, a mother's worst nightmare, was happening to her, and worst of all, she had a suspicion about who was responsible. And if she was right—oh, God, if she was right—her heart slammed against her ribs and she bent double.

If she was right, she might never see her babies alive again.

Somewhere deep inside, she began to silently scream.

"Oh, my dear, how can we help?" Lydia Joyce's lovely voice quavered with emotion. "How old are your girls?"

"They just turned four. In—in July." Maureen barely recognized her own voice. It was high and thin and foreign.

"What can we do? Should we call the police?" Harry Joyce offered.

Maureen didn't want to talk to him. She felt consumed by terror, overwhelmed by the need to act, and act quickly. But what was the best thing to do?

"I'll call them, right away." Again, her voice was harsh and impatient, and she didn't care. Nothing mattered anymore except her twins.

Harry and Lydia Joyce both stared at her.

In her years as a New York police detective, Maureen had witnessed all too often the wild look in victims' eyes when something so horrible happened they could hardly comprehend it. She knew from the shocked expressions on the Joyces' kind faces that that's how she must look at this moment—demented, half mad, out of control. It was how she felt.

"I'm sorry." It wasn't their fault they'd gotten caught up in this disaster.

"Don't you give a thought to us. Just let us know if there's anything we can do."

"I will, thanks." She wanted them to go away. She had to think. She had to—

"Hello, everyone. What's everybody doing out here? And where's that puppy who needs seeing to?"

Maureen swung around at the sound of the hearty, deep male voice, her heart pounding. It took her a dazed moment to even recognize Alex McAlester, the local veterinarian. She'd called him that morning, asking him to drop by and check on Satin, the twins' new puppy, a gift from a young local man.

The puppy seemed healthy enough, but Maureen had wanted to be sure it was free of fleas and could withstand the vigorous loving the twins were already bestowing on it.

The smile on Alex's face faded when he looked at Maureen. He took a step toward her, his hand outstretched.

"Maureen, what's the matter? What's happened?"

She tried to form words, and had to swallow and try again past the tightness in her throat.

"The—the twins—my, my girls, they're—they're go-gone." She could feel panic fluttering in her chest, and fought the desperate sobs that rose in her throat. "It looks as if somebody's kid-kidnapped my twins, Alex." She pulled in a breath and almost choked. "They—whoever it was—they cut the lock off the shed. The girls were hiding in there, playing hide-and-seek with Keegan. There's a bolt cutter in the grass. The lock's there, too. Someone must have—they must have been watching the house. They sneaked down the hillside and—and—they'd have had to drug the girls, or we'd have heard them screaming. They must have wrapped them in something and carried them off—"

She couldn't go on. She'd never fainted in her life, but now the world spun around her in a crazy kaleidoscope of colors. Her legs wouldn't hold her and she sank to her knees, a keening sound of utter desperation coming from her throat as darkness swirled and pulled her down.

"Get your head down." Alex put a huge hand on her skull and gently shoved. Her head dipped close to the earth until the spinning slowed and then stopped.

Maureen heard Lydia Joyce, as if from a far distance, say, "I'll get her a glass of water."

"I'm okay," Maureen said after a few minutes. "I'm okay now." Shaky, still dizzy, she got to her feet, forcing herself to overcome the weakness that pervaded her very bones. She had to think. She had to stop feeling and *think.*

"Thanks." She accepted the water Mrs. Joyce handed her, and forced herself to swallow it as she tried to come up with a plan of action. Almost no one except her immediate family knew of her police background, but it was that training she needed to call upon now.

"Alex, go down to Tubb's Café and find out if anyone saw anything unusual." Cooper's Corner was small, its inhabitants all too aware of strangers. Someone must have seen something. "See if they noticed a strange vehicle, anyone asking about Twin Oaks, anyone or anything suspicious. Hurry, please, Alex."

"Sure thing, Maureen. I'll check at Cooper's Gro-

cery as well—Philo and Phyllis might have seen someone.'' He took off at a dead run.

"Don't disturb anything out here," Maureen
warned the Joyces and Keegan. "I'm going to phone
the police." She wanted one special patrolman, state
trooper Scott Hunter. He was aware of her background
and would know immediately all the ramifications of
this horrible situation.

She ran for the house. Inside the kitchen, she
scanned her list of emergency numbers for the one that
would summon Scott. She had her hand on the phone
when it rang, and a dreadful sense of foreboding came
over her as she snatched up the receiver.

"Hel-hello?" Her voice was trembling, and she
tightened her grip on the receiver until her knuckles
whitened. "Hello?" She could hear breathing.
"Who…who is this?"

"Are you missing something over there, bitch?"
The voice was male, slightly accented, the tone sly.
She'd heard it before, and her heart turned over. "Like
a pair of brats, maybe?"

Maureen swallowed hard, trying to quell the terror
that threatened to overwhelm her.

"Please don't hurt them," she begged. "Please
bring them back. I'll do anything you say, anything.
What is it you want? Just tell me what you want."
The words tumbled out of her, and she fought for
control as the animal on the other end laughed, a
chortle that ended in a high giggle and made her
blood run cold. She'd heard psychotics laugh that
very same way.

"First thing you gotta do is keep your mouth *shut,* mama," he said in a singsong tone. "You say a single word to anybody about this, and the little suckers die, you got that?"

"Yes. Yes, I've got it." Maureen squeezed her eyes shut and bit her lip until she tasted blood, envisioning Alex at this very moment telling everyone in Tubb's Café that the twins were gone.

Oh, God, she should have waited. She should have realized this monster wouldn't want publicity. *Please, God—*

"I promise," she lied. "I won't say a word to anyone. I promise. Just don't hurt them." From some source of strength she didn't know she possessed, she kept her voice from breaking. "I know it's you, Owen Nevil."

"Well, well, so you remember me, do ya? Carl told you I'd get you. You shoulda paid more attention, bitch."

Vivid mental images of Carl Nevil, the murderer she'd helped convict, came clearly to Maureen's mind, and her stomach contracted. His brother Owen was no different.

"We Nevils stick together," he said. "You know what you and that idiot partner of yours did to Carl, but I'm in control here." He laughed again, and Maureen had to swallow hard to keep from gagging.

"You follow orders exactly, mama, or you'll never see your brats alive again. Think about that. I'll be in touch."

"No, no, please, don't hang up—*please—*"

The line went dead. Her knees trembled and once again she couldn't stay upright. She sank down to the tile floor just as the kitchen door burst open.

"What's going on?" It was her distant cousin Philo Cooper. His salt-and-pepper hair stood on end, and his dark eyes were almost popping out of their sockets. "Alex says the twins are gone—that can't be true. He says somebody's kidnapped your girls. Maureen, tell me that's not true!"

Hard on his heels came his plump wife, Phyllis, her shrill voice echoing through the room. "Dear God, I can't believe this is happening. We didn't see a thing. We were in the store all morning, but no strangers came in, did they, Philo?"

"This is terrible, just terrible, Maureen. Did you—" Plump Lori Tubb burst through the door behind Phyllis.

"—call the police?" Her husband, Burt, pot belly jouncing, followed hard on her heels, puffing hard and finishing his wife's sentences just the way Randi and Robin had a tendency to do.

My little girls, where are you?

"What can we do—"

"To help?"

The door opened again, admitting Alex McAlester. "I spread the word, Maureen. Any news yet?"

In the next ten minutes, what seemed to be every last resident of Cooper's Corner crowded into the kitchen. Concerned neighbors and friends poured in through both front and back doors, their kind faces reflecting their horror and distress. As they expressed their shock at the twins' disappearance, their voices rose and fell until Maureen felt she was trapped in a raucous nightmare.

"Maureen, keep your chin up now, we'll get them back. They can't have gotten far." Short and stocky Philo reached up to put a reassuring arm around her shoulders. She could smell sweat, and she knew by the way they were puffing that both Philo and his wife, Phyllis, had run all the way from the general store they operated in the village, not even bothering to take their car.

It was probably because of them that everyone had heard the news. Philo and Phyllis were noted for being the biggest gossips in Cooper's Corner. Nothing escaped them, and nothing stayed secret with them. Maureen knew the couple had good intentions, and she also knew it was an impossibility to ask them not to talk about this.

How would she ever be able to prevent Owen Nevil from knowing that she hadn't kept her word? Panic grew, and Maureen began to lose what few shreds of control she had left.

"Did you call Scott Hunter? Want me to do it for you?" Philo eagerly pulled a cell phone from the pocket of his denim pants.

"No!" Maureen knew she was screaming at Philo, and she didn't care.

"No, put that phone away. You mustn't call the police."

Suddenly the babble of voices died and the kitchen was silent as everyone stood frozen, staring at her.

"No police," she repeated again in a slightly quieter tone. She had to make them understand. They had to realize how important it was that the police weren't notified.

"I had a phone call just now, from the kidnapper. He said—he said—"

Her voice faltered. One glance around the crowded kitchen brought a feeling of utter hopelessness. There were at least fourteen people present already, and more were arriving by the minute.

She looked around at the kind faces of her neighbors and friends and felt panic and utter despair take hold of her.

How could this many people ever keep the twins' disappearance a secret? Helplessness threatened to overwhelm her, but in her mind's eye she saw her babies, frightened, crying for her, and that image gave her strength.

She had to save them. There was no one else, she was their only parent. She *would* save them—anything else was inconceivable. Somehow, she had to convince all these people that they couldn't say a word about what had happened here today.

"Listen to me, all of you, please, *listen.*" Mustering every ounce of strength yet again, she explained to the group about the telephone call she'd just received.

Of necessity, she edited what had been said on the telephone. She didn't want them to know she'd been a New York City police detective. Since moving here she'd used her maiden name and kept quiet about her past life, expressly because of Carl Nevil and his brother, Owen.

She'd been right, she knew that now. But being right was cold comfort when her babies' lives were in danger. Terror nipped at her consciousness like a vicious animal, and she swallowed repeatedly, trying to keep her voice under control.

"The police must not be notified," she emphasized again, registering the doubtful glances her friends and neighbors were giving her and one another. "No one except the people in this room can be told. I beg you all to keep this a secret. Please, please, don't tell a living soul."

A babble of protest broke out.

"He'll murder my babies if he finds out anyone knows." Maureen's cry came from the depths of her soul, and the kitchen grew quiet again.

"We won't say anything, right?" Burt Tubb turned to the crowded room, and heads bobbed in agreement.

Philo and Phyllis, notorious gossips though they were, nodded in unison, and Maureen knew without a doubt that what she was asking was impossible. Inevitably, Owen would hear, and likely the police as well.

Her twins were doomed. The hard knot in her chest burst, and she could no longer hold back the tears.

CHAPTER THREE

"THERE, THERE, MY DEAR. Swallow these, they'll help." Dr. Dorn, a retired doctor who lived in the town, held out several tablets and a glass of water.

Maureen hadn't noticed him until now. The doctor, at least, could keep secrets, but he was outnumbered by those who couldn't.

She shook her head, struggling to regain control. If ever she needed all her wits about her, it was now. Sedatives would make her groggy and thick-headed. She needed all her faculties.

"No," she told the kind old physician. "No sedatives."

Keegan stood beside the doctor, his face pale and stricken. "I'm gonna call my dad, he'll know what to do." He headed for the phone.

"*No.*" Maureen's voice was shrill again, and she drew a shuddering breath. "Keegan, absolutely not. Don't you see. If you call Clint, he'll come back as fast as he can." She tried to soften her sharp tone. "If Clint and Beth race back here from their honeymoon, the kidnapper will know right away that I've talked. You can't call him. And if he should happen to call here, you have to promise me you won't say anything."

Reluctantly, Keegan promised. The boy's face was pale and wan, and he swallowed repeatedly. Maureen could see that his hands were trembling. She took a step toward him, to comfort him, but before she could do anything, the doctor gently took Keegan's arm.

"Come into the other room with me for a minute, son. We need to talk."

Maureen watched them go, grateful that kind Dr. Dorn was able to give Keegan the reassurance he needed, reassurance that she was unable to provide at this moment.

DR. DORN LED KEEGAN INTO the sun porch and gently touched his shoulders, forcing him down to the settee. The old doctor pulled a chair close and sat facing him.

"You're feeling pretty guilty over all this, that right, son?"

Keegan's stomach felt sick, and he hung his head and swallowed hard.

"Yeah. I guess. I mean, it's my fault, right? I was s'posed to be watching them." There was a lump of something stuck in his throat that he couldn't get rid of, no matter how many times he swallowed. He'd had chicken pox when he was four, and he'd thought that was about as sick as a guy could get. His whole body had ached and there wasn't a place that didn't itch. This feeling, though, was about a million times worse.

He'd screwed up, and there didn't seem any way to make it right again.

The last thing he wanted was to cry in front of anybody, but the tears were right there, and he didn't know how long he could hold them back. He dug his nails into his palms to try to localize the pain, but it didn't work.

Dr. Dorn sat back on his chair and expelled a huge sigh. Keegan could smell garlic on his breath, but it wasn't a bad smell.

"Bad things happen, son. And they aren't anybody's fault, they just happen. Only thing we men can do about them is try our best to be strong. Now, I know *you* can do that, you're a tough young man, but I'm worried about your aunt Maureen." Dr. Dorn had a habit of peering over the top of his glasses, his light blue eyes clear and sharp, not missing a thing. He was doing that now.

"I'm afraid she may just break under the strain, Keegan, all alone as she is. She's had a lot to contend with over these past months. Seems like bad luck just keeps following her around. Now, it seems to me she needs family support in all this, and like she said, calling your daddy home isn't a good idea. It would be a certain tip-off to whatever foul scum took the girls. But, Keegan, I've been wondering."

Dr. Dorn tipped his head to the side and frowned.

"I may be way off base here—I don't know anything about Maureen's private life before she came to Cooper's Corner. But I was hoping you might know. Do you have any idea where the twins' father might be? Is he the sort of guy who'd support her in all this? Because if so, it's my opinion Maureen needs him at this moment, regardless of what's gone on between them. He's their daddy, after all. He ought to know what's happening. He should be here to support her.''

Keegan barely heard what the doctor was saying. He was too obsessed with his own sense of guilt. ''Dad told me to take care of Aunt Maureen and the twins for him while he was gone.'' He gulped, hands knotted tight into fists. ''He'll be really, really mad at me.''

''Nonsense, of course he won't.'' The doctor shook his head. ''Don't even think it, boy. Nobody could have guessed that something like this would happen. And in my opinion, nobody can prevent such things. Now, how about it, Keegan? Do you happen to know where the twins' daddy might be? Is there some way we could get hold of him? What's his name, for starters?''

''The twins' dad?'' Keegan hadn't thought about him in a while. He hadn't seen him for a long time, ever since he and Aunt Maureen had split.

''His name's Chance Maguire.''

Keegan had always liked his uncle Chance. He'd seemed to remember what it was like to be a boy, and he'd once taken Keegan out on his sailboat and taught him how to sail. Just thinking about Uncle Chance made Keegan feel a little better. His uncle was a big, strong man, and nothing ever seemed to get to him, from what Keegan could remember. It would be so good to have him here now, to take care of his aunt.

''Think you could get hold of him, Keegan? You have any idea where he works, or where he lives?''

Keegan had heard the grown-ups talking, saying

that Chance had been in Europe but was back in New York now.

"He runs this business that makes tools, it's called Maguire Manufacturing. He has this big office building in New York—he took me there once to see his office and then we went to see the plant. It was a long time ago, I can't remember where it was exactly. And I've never phoned him. I don't know his number."

"Your aunt never seemed afraid of him, did she, son?" Dr. Dorn was doing the glasses thing again. It made him look like a picture Keegan had once seen of Einstein. Doc Dorn had the same white hair, though nowhere near as much, and bushy eyebrows.

"Oh, no. Uncle Chance would never do anything to hurt Aunt Maureen. I don't know exactly why they split up. My dad said it had something to do with my aunt's job and Uncle Chance having to go to Europe. But Aunt Maureen was never scared of Uncle Chance. He's a good guy. He'd never be mean to her or hit her or anything like that."

Keegan didn't know the details of his aunt and uncle's divorce. Who ever knew with grown-ups? He'd learned that they didn't even have all the answers themselves.

"Unusual name, Chance Maguire," Dr. Dorn said. "Can't be too many of them, even in the New York directory. Maguire Manufacturing, you said the company's called? Let's try to track him down there. If we get hold of him, you can tell him what's happened."

Keegan hesitated. The last thing he wanted to do

was make things worse. "Will the kidnappers know we told him? Aunt Maureen wouldn't let me call my dad, because they'd know that she told," he reminded the doctor.

"I think we're safe with the twins' father," Dr. Dorn said. "Way I see it, nobody would blink an eye if he arrived to visit them." The doctor had a cell phone, and within moments he was scribbling down a number on a prescription pad he had in his pocket.

He dialed the number, and in an officious voice, introduced himself, emphasizing that he was a doctor. He winked at Keegan as he did it, as if it was a kind of in-joke just between them.

"My name is Dr. Felix Dorn," he repeated after a moment. "I have Chance Maguire's nephew here with me. He needs to speak with his uncle, it's a matter of some urgency." He listened again, and then said, "Yes, madam, I'll wait. Just don't keep me hanging too long, will you?"

He listened in silence for what seemed a long time.

"Chance Maguire? I have a young man who needs to speak to you on a matter of some urgency."

He handed the phone over to Keegan.

IN NEW YORK, CHANCE MAGUIRE was in the boardroom of his corporate headquarters, in a meeting with his accountants.

There was a serious problem with the plant in England. The chief executive officer, Martin Black, had died suddenly the week before, and his successor, Lindsey Armstrong, had discovered that Black had used company money to invest in the derivatives market.

Chance knew Martin Black, and he understood all too well why the man would do such a thing. Maguire Manufacturing had had problems with sales during the past year. Competition was stiff. High-quality tools were now being made in Korea, and because of labor costs it was becoming more and more difficult to compete on the world market. Martin was inordinately proud of his record as CEO. The English branch of Maguire Manufacturing had never before lost money.

Martin's background was financial, and he'd obviously believed he could buoy up the company's losses by gambling on the commodities market.

Lindsey, the new CEO of the London branch, was moving up from VP Finance, and she'd quickly discovered the slush account. Martin had labeled it an equipment amortization account for punch presses, and Lindsey had immediately realized there was no such thing.

She'd called Chance right away, requesting a special audit of the company's books, and Chance was debating about whom to send over to head up the auditing team.

The obvious choice was his own VP in charge of finance, Wally Shaw. Wally had taken special courses in forensic accounting, and he was also a close friend. He was the logical man for the job.

The problem was, Wally had met Lindsey a few months ago at a seminar in London, and it seemed they hadn't gotten along. In fact, it sounded to Chance as if they'd parted on the worst of terms.

"Armstrong's stubborn, antagonistic and aggressive," Wally declared, his handsome face flushed with emotion. "She's going to block me at every turn, and based on that seminar, I really don't want to ever lay eyes on the woman again. Sorry, Chance, but you'll have to send someone else."

"Strange," Chance remarked, giving Wally a questioning look. "I've always found her agreeable, and totally receptive to any input that's helpful to the company. She's certainly qualified as CEO—she has degrees from the London School of Economics. And she's the one that's requested the audit, Wally. I don't understand your objections."

To the best of Chance's knowledge, Wally had never had personality conflicts with anyone before. He was easygoing, a lanky, good-looking Californian, with the beach boy looks and the laid-back attitude normally associated with the West Coast. He was brilliant in his field. His only weakness was a personal one, an inordinate fondness for the type of women he himself labeled bimbos. He'd never married, and it looked as if he never would, unless he suddenly realized quality was preferable to quantity, and brains had an advantage over breasts.

Chance couldn't help but wonder if there'd been some sort of personal episode between Wally and Lindsey. They were his age, late thirties, both single, attractive. But Wally would never make a move on a business associate, Chance assured himself. Aside from the ethics of the thing, Wally consciously avoided women with anything resembling gray matter when it came to what he mistakenly thought was romance.

"I'd rather not go, Chance," Wally was repeating in a stubborn tone when Stacey, Chance's executive assistant, knocked and then came in.

"Sorry to interrupt, Chance, but there's a call for you from a young man named Keegan Cooper in Cooper's Corner. He says he's your nephew. Someone named—" She consulted a pad of paper in her hand. "—Dr. Felix Dorn made the call for him, and this doctor says it's urgent that the boy speak with you immediately."

Maureen's nephew. Chance hadn't had much contact with any of the Coopers since the divorce. Why would Keegan need to speak to him now?

The very thought of his ex-wife aroused a familiar seething mass of emotions. Chance excused himself and hurried along the corridor and into his office, wondering what this was all about.

He sat down at his desk, took a deep breath and punched in the extension number Stacey had given him, spoke briefly to Dorn, and then waited until a young male voice said a tentative hello.

"Keegan? It's Chance Maguire." Too late, he realized he should have said *Uncle* Chance. Divorce made things so damned difficult on all sorts of levels. He'd been fond of Keegan, and he'd liked and respected Keegan's father, Clint Cooper.

The divorce from Maureen, the bitterness of their

parting had also meant losing an extended family, one that Chance had doubly treasured because he had none of his own. He should have made an attempt to stay in touch with Clint and his family. He'd been in France when word had come of the death of Kristin, Clint's wife. Chance had been shocked and saddened, and he'd written a heartfelt letter to Clint at the time. Clint had responded with a brief, polite note, and Chance hadn't followed up on it.

He cursed himself now for not doing so. He should have made contact when he returned to New York.

"Nice to hear from you," he said now, the warmth and affection he felt evident in his voice. "How are you, Keegan?"

"Hi, Uncle Chance." A deep sigh and then, in a miserable tone, "I'm not very good right now. Something bad happened here."

The boy's voice was thin and strained, and Chance knew at once that something must be terribly wrong. Frowning, he leaned forward in his chair, his gut in a knot.

Maureen. Something must have happened to Maureen.

With an effort, he kept his voice even. "How about telling me what it is, and I'll see what I can do to help?"

"It's the twins, Uncle Chance."

Chance could tell Keegan was fighting back tears.

"They got kidnapped, and I was s'posed to be watching them."

Frowning, Chance shook his head. He had no idea

what Keegan was talking about. All he felt was immense relief that Maureen was all right.

"Hold it, Keegan. You'll have to go a little slower here, you've lost me. Exactly what twins are you talking about?"

The boy's answer brought Chance lurching to his feet.

"*Maureen's* twins?" He felt as if he'd been punched in the gut. It had been four years and eight months since he and Maureen had split.

She'd found someone else and had twins with him?

Resentment gnawed at him. Obviously Maureen hadn't wasted any time in getting on with her life. A welter of memories poured through him, times they'd talked about the babies they'd have together, what they'd call them, what they'd look like.

Anger simmered. Damn her to hell and back. Since their divorce, she'd been able to move on, fall in love, get pregnant, have *twins,* for God's sweet sake, while he hadn't been able to stick to any relationship longer than a month.

Had he even made it through a whole month with any of those women? He couldn't remember, any more than he could remember their faces at this moment.

Twins. He and Maureen used to lie in bed after making love and joke about the possibility that they'd have a set of the twins that ran in Maureen's family. He remembered the feel of her skin, the warmth of her body, the sensation of being one with her.

Apparently she'd shared all that with someone else. Intense jealousy filled him, and with it a twisting heartache for what might have been. And he still couldn't understand why Keegan would be calling him with this garbled story about kidnapping. Why should it matter to him if—

But anything related to Reen mattered to him, he admitted reluctantly. He closed his eyes and thought for a moment.

"Where's the kids' father, Keegan?" he said at last.

Again he listened, and then he sank slowly down into his padded leather chair.

"Can you—Keegan, can you repeat that? I didn't quite—"

Dumbfounded, he tried to assimilate what the boy insisted was so.

Keegan said it again, repeating that *Chance* was the father of the twins. Their names were Randi and Robin, names he and Maureen had long ago agreed on if they had girls.

"How old are they?" This time his voice betrayed something of what he was feeling. It took extreme effort to be patient. He picked up a paperweight, squeezing it so hard the tendons on the back of his hand stood out like tree branches.

Four, Keegan said. They'd turned four in July.

Chance did some quick calculating. It didn't take a mathematician to figure out that Maureen had been four weeks pregnant with them when she and Chance had the final blowup that ended their marriage. Had she known she was pregnant?

She'd never told him. Why hadn't she told him?

A fresh and even more powerful wave of anger

rolled through him. How could she have their babies and never tell him? He'd been a father for four years without knowing of his daughters' existence.

Emotions roiled inside of him. The primary one was a desire to strangle Maureen. And then the full impact of what Keegan was saying hit him like a blow.

"You say they've been kidnapped?"

"I shouldn't have left them alone, Uncle Chance," Keegan said in a voice that trembled. "I went to the bathroom and when I came out they were gone."

Keegan went on talking, explaining over and over that he'd only left them alone for a few minutes, that his aunt Maureen didn't know that he was phoning, that he didn't know what else to do, that Dr. Dorn had said calling Chance was the right thing to do.

"The doctor's absolutely right, Keegan," Chance interrupted. "You did the best thing anyone could do by calling me, and I'm grateful to you. Now, let me talk to the doctor. I need to know exactly where Cooper's Corner is located and where the nearest landing field is. And listen, son, you stop worrying, okay? I'll be there in an hour. Hour and a half, tops. And we'll get the twins back."

Even if he had to marshal the entire U.S. Army, he'd get them back, Chance vowed as he spoke to Dr. Dorn. The first question he asked was whether or not the police had been notified, and Dorn quickly explained why they hadn't.

Chance figured it was a mistake not to call them. Maureen was being foolish, but he'd take that up with her.

Dorn gave him explicit directions, offering to drive to the airfield and meet Chance, then bring him back to Twin Oaks.

Chance accepted with gratitude, and when he hung up, his hands were shaking. He dialed again immediately. Having his own private plane had seemed a rash extravagance at times. Now it was a godsend. Next he called for a car and a driver to take him to the airport.

"Stacey, come with me." He raced along the corridor to the boardroom, his executive assistant puffing along behind him. When he burst through the door, he startled his employees.

"There's a family emergency, and I've got to leave immediately. I don't know how long I'll be gone," he said rapidly. "Wally, I want you to put your personal feelings aside and go to England. I'm relying on you to turn that situation around. Stacey, notify Jim Cornwall that he's in charge here until I get back. Doug, you handle the Cartwright affair, the financing is in order."

Leaving them with their mouths agape, Chance fled out the door again, hurrying to his office to snatch the underwear, clean shirt and socks he kept there and stuff them into a small travel bag. He added a shaving kit from his private bathroom, grabbed his overcoat, and then switched it for a soft and worn leather jacket he'd left at the office some time before.

After a few final words for Stacey, he headed for the elevators, where he banged the control panel and glanced impatiently at his watch.

He'd been generous with the time frame he'd given

Keegan. If the traffic gave him even half a break, he planned to be in Cooper's Corner long before an hour and a half had passed.

But it was going to take time to get control of his temper.

How *could* she have had his children and never told him?

CHAPTER FOUR

MAUREEN GLANCED AT THE CLOCK on the kitchen wall and shuddered. The twins had been gone three hours and ten minutes. She was afraid to leave the house in case Nevil called again, but being here was making her crazy.

She wanted to be alone, to think, to plan, but there was a steady stream of people coming and going.

They came and left again, shocked and wanting to help. They brought casseroles, pies, cakes, cookies. They made fresh coffee, filled pots with herbal tea and set mugs of it in front of her. They patted her shoulder helplessly, assuring her over and over that they hadn't breathed a word to anyone, but how could that be when still more people were arriving who obviously knew all about it? News didn't travel by osmosis.

She should have gone into the small office, where she'd be alone, but some rational part of her just couldn't be rude to those who came to offer sympathy and assistance. So she sat at the kitchen table, unable to do anything except make and discard frantic, unrealistic plans for getting the twins back safe and sound.

She heard the front doorbell ring but ignored it.

There were enough other people around to answer it. It would undoubtedly be yet another neighbor bringing food and assuring her they hadn't told a soul.

She was dimly aware of Keegan's voice, greeting Dr. Dorn. There was a rumble of low male voices, but she paid no attention.

"Hello, Reen."

Her back was to the doorway, and she froze, not looking around.

Only one man had ever called her Reen. She turned slowly, thinking she was hallucinating. For a long moment she was speechless, and then his name came out, no more than a whisper.

"Chance?" She stared up at him, wondering as she had several times these past few hours if this could, after all, be just a horrible nightmare. What other explanation could there be for his appearance here in her kitchen?

For one mindless moment, all she wanted to do was throw herself into his strong, capable arms, but then painful memories intervened. He wasn't her husband or her lover anymore. He was a stranger, a cold-hearted, remote stranger who'd rejected her at a time in her life when she most needed him.

"What are you doing here, Chance?"

She could see that he was angry, although it wouldn't be apparent to anyone who didn't know him as well as Maureen. His midnight-blue eyes met hers directly, but the expression in their depths was cold and forbidding. The faint lines etched between his strong, slightly crooked nose and the corners of his long, narrow, sensual mouth were more pronounced than usual, and a muscle in his square jaw twitched. She was struck all over again by how big he was, tall and broad, towering over the other people in the room.

"I think we have some talking to do, Reen."

There had been at least seven others in the kitchen, but now, just when Maureen would have welcomed their presence, everyone melted away and she and Chance were suddenly alone.

He walked to the cupboard as if he owned the place, found a cup, poured himself coffee from the carafe on the counter.

"Can I get you some fresh?" He gestured at the stoneware cup in front of her.

"It's tea." Gina Monroe, a friend and teacher at the local school, had brewed a potion from herbs that she insisted would calm Maureen's nerves. It tasted like boiled straw, and after the first mouthful, she hadn't touched it. Maybe she should have, because at this moment she felt that screaming her lungs out at this man would be an appropriate response.

"Do you want more?"

She shook her head. He sat down at the table, and Maureen stared across at him. It had been nearly five years since she'd last laid eyes on him. There were new lines around his deep-set eyes and sensual mouth, and the odd gray hair stood out amid his thick, blue-black curls.

He was older, but the charisma that had attracted her the very first time she'd met him was as strong as ever. Chance gave off sexual energy the way other men exuded after-shave. She'd always wondered if every woman he met was affected by it, or if it was something that happened only to her.

"What—what are you doing here, Chance? How did you find out—" Her throat closed up and she had to swallow hard.

"About my children? Keegan called me."

Maureen felt amazed and resentful that her nephew would take it on himself to call Chance.

"He had no right to do that."

"He didn't do it all on his own, Reen. It was the doctor's suggestion. But regardless of who thought of it, I'm very glad it happened." He sipped his coffee and in the same level tone said, "Now, I think it's time for you to tell me exactly what's happened to *our* daughters."

He was furious with her. She knew the signs, knew them all too well from having lived with him for the fourteen months their marriage had lasted. Chance never showed anger by stomping around or yelling. Instead, he grew quiet and very still, the way he was right now, looking at her with eyes like hard blue stones, his features impassive, a tiny muscle in one cheek twitching.

His lack of visible emotion had always driven her in the opposite direction. She'd responded to his controlled anger with loud sarcasm, hollering, once even throwing a hardcover book at him in utter, absolute frustration. It had missed him and hit a window, shattering it. They'd ended up laughing, cleaning up the glass together and then making love with all the passion left over from the quarrel.

Right now she had no energy to spare for such histrionics. She drew in a shaky breath and, as if she were reading from a police report, gave him the bare details of the kidnapping.

He shook his head, frowning, and his impatience showed in his tone. "I don't understand. This is obviously a quiet, backwoods little town. Who the hell would do a thing like this, and why?"

Maureen glanced around. The kitchen was deserted for the moment, but she didn't want anyone overhearing what she'd gone to such lengths to keep private.

"And why the *hell* haven't you called the police?"

"I was about to when the kidnapper phoned. Come into the office and we'll talk." If a call came from Nevil, she'd be able to take it on the extension there.

She led the way down the winding passageway to the small office Clint had created underneath the stairs.

Maureen sat down behind the desk, uncomfortably aware of the cramped space and the size of her former husband. Chance was four inches over six feet, with wide shoulders and a large, muscular frame that made the tiny space seem even smaller than it was.

He perched on the only other chair in the room, a plain, high-backed antique wooden one that was anything but comfortable, despite the thick maroon cushion Maureen had sewn for it.

It looked as if it might collapse under his weight.

Good, she thought rebelliously. When his ass hit the

refinished oak floor, maybe he'd lose that iron control and really show how mad he was for once.

But the chair held, and he was again giving her that level look of his, raising one thick black eyebrow questioningly.

"Tell me how this came about, Reen."

The intimacy of his pet name for her only emphasized to Maureen how far apart they really were.

"Did you ever hear Dan and I talk about a nasty piece of work named Carl Nevil?" Dan had been her partner the whole time she'd been a detective. She missed him so much. She'd give anything to have him at her side right this moment.

Chance thought about it and shook his head. "I don't remember that particular name."

"We finally arrested him, and at his trial he was convicted of the murder of a police officer. He was given life, and Dan and I were in the courtroom when the sentence was handed down." Even now, Maureen got chills when she remembered. She shivered and wrapped her arms around her breasts.

"Nevil threatened us. He swore that Dan and I and the informer who tipped us off would be taken care of." She gave a weary shrug. "Dan and I were used to it. The difference with Carl Nevil was that he had a brother who was willing to carry out his threats. Owen Nevil had been serving time for conspiracy to commit murder, and he was granted parole about the time Carl was sentenced."

Chance waited silently, his icy-blue eyes steady on Maureen's face.

"A week after Owen Nevil's release, our informant was struck down and killed when he was crossing the street. It was hit and run. Nevil was brought in for questioning, but there was no evidence to prove that he was the one behind the wheel. Dan and I were present when he was questioned, and I just knew he was guilty, I felt it in my gut."

Chance was watching her, listening to every word.

"When he looked at me—I can't explain it—it was almost vicious. That look sent ice through my veins. He has these eyes, so dark it's like you're gazing into the pits of hell." She thought of her helpless babies, at Nevil's mercy, and had to struggle once again with hysteria. It took a moment to compose herself.

"Just about that time, my great-uncle died and willed Twin Oaks to Clint and me," she went on. "It seemed a heaven-sent opportunity for a saner, safer life. Clint had lost Kristin, and Keegan was acting out, hanging with a bad crowd, using profanity, being rebellious. Clint was really worried about him. And Dan was retiring, which meant a new partner for me. Nevil's threats might not have bothered me if it hadn't been for the twins. It's one thing to risk your own life, but it's quite another when you have kids."

Chance's blue eyes darkened as his anger grew. "I can't believe you didn't even bother to let me know that *I* had kids."

That wasn't something she wanted to get into right now, so she ignored his remark. "Clint and I decided to come here and start a B and B. We didn't have any idea how much work was involved, which was probably a good thing or we might have decided against it. Anyway, when I moved here, I used my maiden name, and Frank Quigg—you remember Frank, my superior officer?''

Chance did. He'd liked Frank.

''Well, Frank kept an eye on Owen Nevil until I could move out of town, and then he sealed my departmental records so no one could learn my maiden name or place of birth and be able to track me down.''

''But in spite of all that, you figure Nevil found you here, that it's him who's taken the twins.''

She nodded, and the pain she'd managed to put at bay for a few moments came back. ''I know it's him. Just before you arrived, he called me and told me that he has them, and that no one else is to know.''

Chance shook his head. ''But there were a dozen people in the house when I got here, all of whom—''

Maureen nodded. ''They all know. Half the countryside knows, and the other half is probably hearing about it right now.'' She gave her head a hopeless shake. ''The vet came by just as I realized the twins were gone. I sent him over to the café to see if anyone had noticed anything. He went from there to the general store, and the word spread like a fire fed by gasoline. And—and then Nevil phoned, warning me to keep quiet or—or...'' She gulped and her face contorted.

''Or what?'' Chance's voice was very quiet.

''Or he'd kill the twins.''

Chance's eyes narrowed, and a hard, implacable expression tightened his mouth. The muscles in his jaw stood out. "I still think we should call the police. If half the village knows, why not the police?"

"*No.* Not the police, absolutely not."

He must have sensed that he'd get nowhere with that, because he dropped it and said next, "How long have they been gone?"

"Three hours and forty-five minutes now," Maureen said with a glance at the wall clock.

"Do you have any pictures of them?" There was a yearning in his voice that made her forget her resentment of him.

Late at night, after the twins were asleep and she was too exhausted to sleep herself, she'd sometimes imagined Chance appearing this way, meeting his daughters. Never in her worst nightmares could she have imagined the circumstances under which her fantasy would come true.

She got up and went into the living room for a moment, retrieving the photo albums she'd kept from the day the girls were born. Back in the office, she silently handed them to Chance.

He opened the first album and she saw his jaw tense. She noticed the way he swallowed hard as he slowly turned the pages, and she knew he was recognizing himself in the babies' identical smiles, their long-fingered hands, the pronounced cleft in their tiny chins, an exact replica of the one in his own stubborn chin.

Tears burned behind her eyes. Despite their differences, she and Chance had been united in their desire for children. During the early days of their marriage, they'd spent so many hours talking about the family they'd have.

"They're beautiful, Reen." The anger was gone. He sounded as if he, too, was on the verge of tears. "I could never have imagined how perfect they are."

"They are, aren't they?" She'd never realized quite how much she'd longed to share this rush of parental pride with Chance. She knew that even her fantasies had been interlaced with resentment. It had been impossible to get past how bitter she felt toward him.

But at this moment, all that negative emotion was gone. As he turned the pages of one album after the other, she saw her own tenderness and absolute wonder at the beauty of their babies reflected in his eyes.

"Which is which? How do you tell them apart? They're so very much alike."

"This is Randi, that's Robin. And when you're around them a lot, you couldn't possibly get them mixed up. They each have their own little ways." Her voice quavered. "I'd say Randi is more like you, Robin like me."

He listened, and when he looked over at her, it was with a silent recognition that together they'd created these precious little ones.

There was no resentment, no blame in his look this time. She understood that whatever the issues were between her and Chance, they'd silently, mutually agreed for this one moment in time to put them aside.

"Whatever there's been between us, Reen, we obviously managed to do this one thing right. And now all that matters is getting these babies back safely."

His words were husky and heartfelt. "I'll do whatever it takes, Reen. I'll give everything I have in this world, including my life."

She swallowed back tears and nodded agreement. "Me, too." She allowed herself to try to imagine where they were, what might be happening to them. Were they hungry? Had they been heavily drugged? She gave a small, soft moan at the thought that her babies were hurting, crying for her.

"We have to concentrate on the end result, Reen." Chance's voice was unusually soft, even tender. "Imagine how great it's going to be when we get them back."

She tried, but the dark images were too powerful.

CHAPTER FIVE

BILLY KNEW THE LITTLE GIRLS had been given a powerful drug. When Angie carried them in and dumped them on the bed in his room, he'd heard her say she hoped they'd had a decent dose so they'd sleep a good long while. She didn't want to be bothered with squalling brats.

One thing Billy had learned since he came to live with Angie Spratt was that she had no use for kids. He tried to keep out of her way as much as he could, but it was a small apartment.

He was grateful that school had started again. At least it got him away from Angie for a long time each day. Today the teachers were having meetings, though. Angie had been out all morning, so he'd been home on his own, and he was there when she and his brother Owen got back. She'd carried one of the little girls in and Owen had carried the other. They'd dumped them like little sacks on his bed.

"You can make yourself useful for a change," Angie had snarled at Billy. "You keep an eye on these two, and when they wake up, you keep them quiet. I'm worn out. I'm gonna watch my soaps, and I don't want no kids howlin' so I can't hear myself think."

Billy was nine. He was small for his age, but he still figured by the size of them, he was probably lots older than these little girls. He spent a long time looking at them, amazed by how much alike they were. He hadn't ever been around twins, not close up. There were some at the school he went to, but they weren't exactly alike the way these two were. He wondered where Owen had gotten them. He'd probably stolen them; Owen stole lots of things.

They had on small blue running shoes and white socks, blue shorts and blue shirts. One of them was lying on her back, and Billy saw that there was something red on the front of her little shirt.

He thought at first it was blood, but when he really looked he could see it wasn't. It was maybe tomato soup or something. He reached out and gently touched their rich brown curls with his fingers, fascinated by how soft and clean their hair felt and how it wrapped itself around his fingers.

They were awfully small, and their faces were pale. There were dark circles under their eyes, and he figured maybe that came from whatever was making them sleep like this. Their tiny hands fascinated him. He lifted first one and then another, looking at the pudgy fingers, the dimples on the back.

He watched them for what seemed a very long time. The slit of sunshine that came in the narrow window was already halfway up the wall, which meant it was way past noon. It made him feel bad to see how still they stayed. He shoved his pillow under their heads and covered them with his sour-smelling quilt, but they didn't move on their own.

Finally Billy got bored with looking at them. He sat down in the corner of the room on the floor and played with the small computer game his sister had given him, but he wasn't really concentrating. He was waiting for the babies to wake up.

He got scared after a while and thought maybe they were dead. He'd seen a show on TV once where that happened, where they gave a little kid too much stuff to keep him quiet and the kid died.

Frightened, he went over and put his head down close to their faces, and was reassured when he felt how warm they were. He could even smell their quiet breath, a little milky and sour with sleep.

It wasn't long after that before one of them wriggled and rubbed her eyes, then pushed her bum up under the quilt. She made a little whining sound, and a few moments later she finally sat up.

She rubbed her eyes with her fists and then she looked around. She had big eyes, the color of blue and green mixed together. Her square little face was all marked from the wrinkles in the pillowcase, and the first thing she searched for was her sister. She put a hand on her twin's head and noticed Billy next, her eyes wide and scared-looking.

Her mouth turned down and her face puckered. She was about to howl. Billy didn't want to rush over and scare her even more.

"Hi, little girl." He talked quietly and waved a hand at her, smiling.

She ducked her chin and gave him a suspicious stare from under her long lashes. She pouted, but at least she didn't start crying.

"What's your name, girl? I'm Billy."

He went on smiling, and she looked at him for a while longer. Then she put one hand on each side of her sister's face, leaning over and whispering to her, trying to wake her up.

"What's your name?" he asked again. Maybe she was too little to know.

"Ro-bin," she whispered.

He didn't catch it. "Tell me again."

"Ro-bin." Her voice was louder now.

He put the two parts together. "Hi, Robin. What's your sister's name?"

"Ran-di."

"Randi and Robin." He'd never heard those names before, but they seemed good names for twins.

"Randi. Up now." Robin went on patting until, gradually, the other twin woke. She sat up, too, and looked around, her big eyes dazed, but then she started crying almost right away, rubbing her eyes and wailing at the top of her lungs.

"Mama," she sobbed. *"Maaa—maaa."* Her voice rose to an imperious bellow. *"Maaa—maaa."*

"Sh. Hey, shut up, kid. Angie's gonna get real mad at us." Billy went over to her, but she cried even harder. He offered her his game, and she batted it away with her little hand.

He felt sorry for her. He knew how it felt, being dumped places where people didn't want you and you didn't know anybody. But he was also anxious, because Angie got real mean when she wanted to watch her soaps and there was noise.

He tried to make faces for Randi, but she wouldn't look at him. And then the other twin started crying, too, just as loud, and in another minute the bedroom door slammed open and Angie came storming in.

"You shut up that howlin', or so help me I'll give you somethin' to howl about," she shouted at the twins, holding her hand up as if she intended to smack them.

The twins gave her one look and wrapped their arms around each other, but then they really started screaming loud.

Billy felt awful when Angie hauled off and smacked them. She hit them on their legs, and they shrieked. Angie threatened them again, and after that, to Billy's relief, they stopped crying out loud. They still sobbed and clung to each other, but they swallowed the sound back, the same way he'd learned to cry when he was little.

But he was big now and didn't cry much anymore. Only at night when he thought about his sister and wished he could be with her. He always buried his head in the pillow, so nobody could hear.

"Now, you do what I told you—you keep them quiet, you hear me?" Angie turned her anger on Billy, and he was scared but he was also glad. He was used to her. She always said she'd beat him black and blue, but so far she hadn't done more than cuff him on the head. Except for that one time he'd had the bad dream and screamed and screamed. She'd taken the belt to him that time for waking her up in the middle of the night.

She swore and then stormed out, and Billy quickly dug his secret stash of cookies out of his backpack and held one out to each twin. They stopped sobbing and warily accepted the treat, and he could tell by the way they gobbled them down that they were hungry. He knew they should have milk—babies always drank milk—but he didn't dare go to the fridge. He'd gotten in trouble for that before. Angie was real strict about not taking food between mealtimes. Sometimes if she was really interested in her shows, though, he could sneak out and get something.

He went in the bathroom and got a glass of water, and sure enough, they were real thirsty. He was surprised at how good they were about sharing. One twin waited until her sister had drunk some before reaching out for the glass, and they handed it back and forth. He couldn't really tell them apart, now that they were both up and moving around.

"I have to go pee-pee," one of them whispered next, and he helped her off the bed and started toward the door. But the other one began crying again, so he quickly lifted her down, too, and with one of their hands in each of his, they headed down the hall to the bathroom. It was a good thing the girls hadn't peed on the mattress; that was what happened when he'd had the bad dream. He'd been so ashamed of himself that time, he'd hardly felt it when Angie used the belt on him.

Billy was relieved to find that they were okay about pulling down their own shorts and going by themselves. He didn't know much about how girls did stuff like that. His sister was real private about such things. He stood outside the door and waited until he figured they were done. He could hear Angie talking on the phone in an irritated voice.

"You better make it quick. Brats that age are nothing but work. I'm not running a home for orphans here." She listened and then said, "Yeah, well, I agreed to one night, but then you come and get them."

Billy felt relieved. It sounded as if Owen would be taking the twins back to their mother tomorrow. But in the meantime, he'd have to figure out some way of keeping them quiet.

Maybe later they could watch cartoons, when Angie's soaps and the millionaire shows she liked to watch were over. She sometimes let him watch for a while, if she was in a good mood.

Or he could read them stories. He had a couple of books with little kids' stories in them. His sister had given them to him, and he kept them in the bottom of his backpack. He'd wait until Angie was into her soaps again, and then he'd try and sneak some crackers and peanut butter from the kitchen.

"All done, Billy," a small voice announced, and he grinned down at the little girl, pleased that she'd remembered his name. Her shorts were pulled up crooked and her shirt wasn't tucked in, so he did his best to fix her up. There was a red mark on her leg where Angie had smacked her, and it made Billy sad. Nobody should hit little kids like these.

Her cheeks were rosy, and he touched her curly hair again. It was soft as the fur on the newborn puppy he'd stroked when the mutt downstairs had a litter.

"Billy, are you our cousin, like Keegan?"

He didn't know what she meant, and he shook his head. "Nope, I don't think so."

"Keegan plays hide and seek with us." Her lip trembled. "We want Keegan. Can we go home now, Billy?"

Her sister came out of the bathroom just then, and two pairs of huge blue-green eyes looked up at him.

"We want our mommy. Where is Mommy?" Their mouths turned down. Tears gathered and began to drip down their cheeks, and he knew that in another moment they'd be howling and Angie would hit them again.

"C'mon, let's go make a cave with the quilt and we can hide in it, sort of like hide and seek, okay?" He led them back into his bedroom and shut the door.

Too bad there wasn't a real cave where they could all hide. It was hard work, keeping little kids from crying. It was going to be tough taking care of them until tomorrow. He wondered if Angie would let him take them outside. He figured probably she wouldn't, not if they were stolen. And he couldn't go out himself and leave them, that wouldn't be fair. But it meant he'd be around when Owen came for them.

Billy shuddered. He hated being around when Owen came.

He hated Owen. He wished the police had kept him in jail like they did Carl, but they'd let him go. Billy had thought sometimes of going to the police and telling them about what Owen did to him and his sister, but he figured they probably wouldn't care, and then Owen would find out and be really, really mad. Nope, it was better to stay away from the police.

"WE HAVE TO CALL THE POLICE, Reen." Chance tried once again to make her see reason. "How else are we going to find them?"

"No." She shook her head, chin up and mouth set in that determined way he remembered so well. "Absolutely not. I won't endanger the twins that way."

He held on to his temper, but only barely. "How exactly do you intend to find them if you don't notify the authorities that they've been kidnapped? We can't do this ourselves."

"We can't tell the police. I told you before, Nevil said on the phone that—that if I told anyone, he'd kill them."

"How would he find out?"

"I've thought for a long time that he must have an informant planted here in town, someone who tells him where I am and what I'm doing. Whoever it is could have already told him that people know. But if by some miracle that person hasn't heard, and I notify the police, then they'll know for certain."

Chance saw the way she struggled for control, and he felt a wave of admiration and sympathy for her. She was brave, the bravest woman he'd ever known.

And the most stubborn. She'd always had the ability to drive him to distraction because of the way she made up her mind and then refused to change it.

"For God's sake, Reen, half the village already knows, you said so yourself. If there is an informant, he's bound to hear what everyone's talking about. And it's only a matter of time until somebody tells the police, anyway. We ought to do it ourselves, right now, before any more time goes by."

"No, Chance." She got up and walked over to stand close to him, looking up into his face, jade-green eyes pleading for understanding.

"People found out before I had an opportunity to do anything to keep it quiet. I had no control over that. But I do over this. When I was NYPD, I couldn't understand why people didn't immediately call the authorities when something like this happened. But I do now. I can't risk my babies' lives. Please, please try to understand."

"*Our* babies," he corrected, but he did it gently.

"Our babies," she agreed, and he saw the stubbornness in the way she held her mouth, but he also saw the vulnerability in her eyes.

"Why didn't you ever tell me about them?" The accusation burst out of him. He'd vowed not to confront her, not now, when she was distraught. But he couldn't help himself. He simply had to know.

"I tried." She looked away. "You wouldn't take my phone calls."

He opened his mouth to deny it, and saw the worry

and weariness in her eyes. He'd been right before—this wasn't the time or the place.

"Give me your word, Chance. Give me your word you won't go behind my back and call the police."

He didn't respond. He still didn't think it was the right decision.

"Chance, there've been attempts on my life since I moved here to Cooper's Corner. This—this scum who has our babies, he's not just threatening. He'll do it, Chance. He'll kill them if we don't do exactly what he says."

"Attempts on your life?" That made him furious. It made him feel helpless. It made him want to rip someone apart with his bare hands. "Tell me exactly what happened."

But before she could answer, there was a tap on the office door.

Maureen opened it.

Phyllis Cooper stood there, her light green eyes filled with alarm.

"Maureen, Scott Hunter's here." She winked madly, looking as if she'd developed a serious tic. "I told him about the *potluck.*"

"I'll be right there." Maureen closed the door and sagged against it.

"Oh, my God." Her breath came in short gasps. "I knew this would happen. Somebody's told Scott, and now the police know, and Nevil's—Nevil's going to—to kill them."

"Who's Scott Hunter?"

"He's a state trooper."

Chance had wanted the police to know, but now he was no longer sure it was a good idea. He wasn't sure of anything anymore, except that he needed to support Maureen in any way he could.

"Let's go out and talk to him. I'll come with you."

SCOTT HUNTER, TALL AND LANKY, was waiting in the front hall, uniform cap in hand, coffee-colored hair clipped close to the scalp in military style.

"Hi, Maureen," he greeted her, his gaze going past her to focus on Chance, who was right behind her. "Thought I'd drop by and bring you these tickets to the ball game next Sunday. We're playing the volunteer firemen. Laurel's going. She thought maybe you'd come along and help her cheer us on. There's a barbecue afterward at our place, and we'd like you to come."

He didn't know.

For a long moment, Maureen couldn't reply as relief coursed through her. She struggled to control her expression, to keep any of her feelings from showing on her face.

She didn't succeed, because Scott looked from Chance to her and frowned, his kind face concerned.

"Anything wrong, Maureen?" He shot another glance at Chance. "You okay?"

"Yes—I mean no," she stuttered. "Nothing's wrong. I'm just a little, uh, distracted." Belatedly, she realized he was waiting for her to introduce him.

"Scott, this is my—my former husband, Chance Maguire."

Chance stepped forward and extended his hand. He was an imposing figure, two inches taller than the policeman.

"How do you do, Scott?"

Scott took his hand and gave a curt nod.

Maureen saw his expression change when he found out Chance was her ex. Scott had been trying to line her up with his friend and fellow patrolman, Duff Sperling. Duff had asked her out several times, and she'd finally accepted a dinner date two weeks before. He was a perfectly nice man, divorced, rugged-looking, intelligent. But after the first hour, she'd known he just wasn't right for her. She'd gently explained that she'd decided not to become involved with anyone until the girls were older, but he'd refused to give up. He'd called her twice, and she knew he'd be playing on the ball team on Sunday, and that he'd also be at the barbecue, watching for her.

"Where are the twins?" They loved Scott and usually mobbed him when he arrived at the door. He always brought them sugarless gummy bears as a treat.

Scott's question sent new panic shooting through Maureen.

"They're—they're having a nap." She hoped that it was true, that somewhere her babies were sleeping innocently, warm and cared for. She also hoped that Scott didn't notice the way she had to swallow hard at the lump in her throat.

"Well, tell them hi from me and give them these." He handed over a small bag, and there was a long, awkward pause. "Guess I'll be going, then," he said at last. "Phyllis said you're having a potluck here to-night. Guess you're kinda busy."

Maureen could hear muted voices in the kitchen.

"Oh, yes, it's a spur of the moment thing." She knew he was waiting for an invitation. She always included him and Laurel in any celebration at Twin Oaks, and when it didn't come, she could see that he was disappointed.

"Thanks for the tickets, Scott."

"Nice to meet you, Maguire." His tone was curt.

Chance closed the door after him and blew out a long breath.

"He didn't know."

The amazement and relief Maureen felt was echoed in Chance's tone.

Phyllis peered around the doorway, and when she saw that Scott was gone, she came hurrying over to Maureen, her chubby face creased in a worried frown.

"I hope that was okay, dear, saying that about the potluck. I didn't know what else to do. He gave me such a start, standing at the door in his uniform that way, and after you warning us, I just couldn't tell him the truth, could I?"

"It was the right thing to do, Phyllis."

"Philo's gone back to the store. It looks fishy if we leave it closed longer than an hour or so. I should go back myself and lend a hand." Her eyes filled with tears. "I just wish there was something more we could do for you. Those poor, sweet babies."

Just don't tell anyone, Maureen wanted to beg. But she'd already said it several times over. There wasn't any point repeating it. And with Phyllis, it was probably like asking her not to breathe.

Soon after Phyllis left, the other neighbors also went home, leaving the house empty except for Maureen and Chance and the Joyces, who'd gone up to their room. Chance and Maureen once again sat down in the kitchen.

Maureen's eyes darted to the clock. "It's almost four." She smashed her hand down on the wooden table, rattling cups and slopping cold coffee on the polished oak.

Her voice was agonized. "*Why* doesn't he phone?"

CHAPTER SIX

CHANCE WAS ONCE AGAIN MADE aware of the narrow edge Maureen was balancing upon emotionally. He'd never seen her like this.

"There must be other things we can do while we wait," he suggested. "Surely someone in this village noticed something unusual, a strange car, a man who looked like Nevil...."

He knew he was grasping at straws, but at least it might distract Maureen, give her something to do besides sit and wait for a phone call.

She shook her head. "No one seems to have noticed anything. It's fall, the leaves are turning. Any other season, strangers stand out, but not at this time of the year."

"Tourists?"

"Just people looking at the scenery."

"Cooper's Corner and the surrounding countryside *are* spectacularly beautiful, Maureen. I wasn't in the mood to appreciate scenery on the flight up, but you'd have to be blind not to notice those trees. From the air, they look like they're on fire."

"There's a steady stream of leaf-peepers passing through town. With so many cars and people, the villagers stop paying attention."

Frustration was nearly killing him. He wanted to do something, take action. "What about the bolt cutters? Didn't you say you'd found the bolt cutters that were used to cut the chain on the gate?"

"Keegan found them. If I package them, could you mail them off to Frank? I don't want to leave the house in case the phone rings."

"Get them ready, tell me where the nearest FedEx outlet is, and I'll do it right away."

"The local gift shop has a courier service. It's probably a useless effort, though. I doubt there're fingerprints on them." Maureen sounded disheartened. "Nevil's too professional to leave any trace. But we'll send them, anyway. I'll just tell Frank my property was broken into, ask if he can run the prints against Owen's."

"Hi, Uncle Chance." Keegan came hesitantly through the sliding doors and into the kitchen, a redheaded, rawboned boy right behind him. Keegan was carrying a puppy, and he set it down now.

"Hello, Keegan. Hi, Trevor." Maureen attempted a smile.

"Hi, Ms. Cooper," the boy said. "Keegan told me what happened. I'm sure sorry about the twins."

Keegan shot Maureen a guilty look. Chance knew he was remembering what she'd said about not telling anyone.

"This is my uncle Chance, Trev—he's the girls' dad," Keegan explained in a rush. "Aunt Maureen, just after Trevor was finished delivering papers this morning, he saw a van on the road just below the house. The reason I told Trev in the first place was because he's always out before anybody in the morning. I thought he might have noticed somebody hanging around."

Maureen focused all her attention on the boy. "What kind of van? Did you happen to notice the license plate, Trevor?"

Trevor shook his head. "Sorry, Ms. Cooper. I don't remember the numbers, except I did notice it wasn't local. I think it was from New York, but I can't be sure. Anyhow, it was old, a dark gray color. A woman was driving."

"You did really well to notice as much as you did, Trevor. Did you get a good look at the woman at all?"

Again, the boy shook his head. "I just noticed she was sorta old. She had that kinda phony yellow hair that doesn't look real. She didn't stop or anything, just drove up and down the road kinda slow. I figured she was looking at the leaves on the hill behind your house."

"How old would you guess she was, Trevor?" It obviously took a huge effort for Maureen to smile at him, but Chance noticed that she managed it. "Old as me? Or old like your grandma Vine?"

He admired the way Maureen questioned the boy. Desperate as she was, she kept her voice calm, and she was careful not to make Trevor feel pressured.

Trevor screwed up his face in an effort to remember, as if his thought process was attached to his facial muscles. "I'd say younger than Grandma, but older than you, Ms. Cooper."

"So maybe in her forties, early fifties," Maureen concluded. "Did you happen to notice anything else, Trev? Anything at all, even if it doesn't seem important."

Trevor screwed up his face again and thought about it, but after a moment he shook his head. "That's about it. I'm sure sorry. I wish now I'd looked more careful."

"You did wonderfully well to even notice the van, Trevor. Thank you more than I can say for telling us. What time would that have been?"

"Because there was no school, I was late with the papers. They take me about an hour, so I'd say it was nine already, maybe a little after."

"That would be about the right time. And Trevor?"

"Yes, ma'am?"

"If you really want to help, the thing I need you to do is keep this a secret. You mustn't tell anyone else about it, okay?"

"Oh, no, Ms. Cooper. I already promised Keegan I wouldn't say a word." He hesitated. "Well, except for my mom and dad. I already told them. I hope you don't mind."

Chance knew how very much she *did* mind. The Vines were two more people who knew, two more breaks in the promise she'd made to Nevil not to say anything. But again, she smiled. "That's absolutely okay. Of course you had to tell your parents. Just please ask them not to say anything, not to anyone. The twins—"

Her voice trembled and threatened to break. She

cleared her throat. "See, Trevor, whoever took the twins told me that if anyone found out about it, the girls would—would die."

Trevor's chocolate-brown eyes widened, and this time he forgot to stop nodding. "Keegan told me that, too," he said in an awed tone. "Don't you worry, Ms. Cooper, nobody else will find out, not from me." He made a zipping motion with his fingers across his mouth.

"Thank you, Trevor." Maureen waved a hand at the cupboard, loaded down with cinnamon buns and cookies and muffins that people had brought. "Now, why don't you boys eat as much of this food as you can hold? There's milk in the fridge to wash it down with."

"Awesome," Trevor breathed, eyeing the bounty. "Thanks, Ms. Cooper."

Chance noticed that although Trevor ate his way through two buns, a muffin, a handful of cookies and several scones, Keegan didn't touch a thing.

The boy's face was pale, his shoulders slumped. Chance watched him as he found a saucer and put water down for the puppy, and then fed it some biscuits from a bag in the pantry.

Walking over to him, Chance put a hand on Keegan's shoulder and gave it a reassuring squeeze, which earned him a grateful look from eyes that seemed too world-weary and sad to belong to a teenager.

"Your pup?" Chance bent over to stroke the fat little ball of fur. The puppy immediately whined and rolled over on its back so he could pat its round, bare little belly.

"She belongs to the girls," Keegan said. "Her name's Satin."

"They'll be grateful to you when they get home for taking such good care of her," Chance said. "Can we rely on you to watch out for her? Maybe take her into your room with you tonight, so she isn't too lonely?"

Chance suspected it was Keegan who'd need the comfort of having the little dog close.

Keegan gave a laconic nod. "Sure, Uncle Chance. I'll make sure she's fed and I'll put some papers down for her on my floor. She's not totally trained yet."

"Thanks, son. Everyone's distracted, and unless you take charge of her, she's liable to get herself into trouble. You know what puppies are like."

He gave Keegan a conspiratorial smile, knowing from experience that having a job to do would help take the boy's mind off his own feelings.

It was all too obvious that Keegan felt responsible for what had happened.

The afternoon crept slowly past with no further word from the kidnappers. Maureen packaged the bolt cutters and the lock, and following Maureen's directions, Chance walked with them to the gift shop.

He explained to the tiny woman behind the counter that the package needed to go out as soon as possible.

"It'll be in New York by tomorrow morning," she assured Chance. "Larry'll be here in twenty minutes for the courier bag."

She weighed the box and Chance paid, signing his name on the invoice, putting Twin Oaks as his address.

The woman gave him a keen look and glanced around. There were no other customers at the counter.

A young woman with scarlet hair was putting out a display of wizened-apple dolls on a shelf, and an elderly woman who'd been looking at a display of greeting cards went out the door, calling, "Can't make up my mind. I'll come back later, Edna."

"Bye, Caroline." The tiny woman waved a hand and then leaned forward, her pouter-pigeon breasts resting on the counter. She lowered her voice to a stage whisper. "You must be the Cooper twins' daddy, am I right?"

Chance nodded. How the hell did she know? Maureen had reverted to using her maiden name, a fact that hurt him more than he'd let on.

"My name is Edna Fisher. My sister Mary and I own the store. Mary's off sick today," she hissed at Chance. "Philo came by and told me what happened, said the baby's daddy was here to take charge."

"I'm Chance Maguire. Pleased to meet you, Edna." It still felt strange to be called a daddy, stranger still when he hadn't laid eyes on his daughters.

"Poor, poor wee mites." She shook her head and pushed up her glasses with a forefinger. "There's not much we can do, stuck in here all day, but Mary and I want you to know we're praying hard for all of you. And if we see anything suspicious, we'll call Twin Oaks right away. We know about not telling the police.'' She made a tapping motion on her lips, signifying silence.

It seemed that everyone knew everything except the police, Chance thought with a sinking feeling. He thanked Edna and turned to leave. He was despondent, at a loss as to what to do next, yet at the same time he felt an overwhelming sense of urgency.

The young woman with the shocking red hair gave him a long, speculative look as he walked past her. She had strange eyes, such a light, clear gray they seemed transparent.

Back at Twin Oaks, a fresh stream of villagers came and went, bringing chicken casseroles, salads, loaves of homemade bread, apple pies, tureens of soup and more cookies and cakes and buns than Chance had ever seen in one kitchen at the same time. There wasn't a spare inch of counter left.

With each delivery of food came an assurance to Maureen that the bearer hadn't breathed a word to anyone. Somehow, however, word had spread that Chance was the twins' daddy, and one after another, the men in the village took him aside and offered to back him up in any way necessary, should he need it.

The most touching gesture came from Philo Cooper, a stocky middle-aged man who was married to Phyllis, whom Chance had already met. When Philo arrived, Maureen had gone to the bathroom and there was a lull in the influx of neighbors, so Chance introduced himself.

Philo shook his hand and then glanced around the kitchen. He jerked a thumb toward the hallway and led the way into the wood-paneled library, its walls packed floor to ceiling with books.

After shutting the door, Philo carefully inspected the room to be certain they were alone. He then reached into the voluminous pocket of his jacket and pulled out a gun.

"This was my father's. She's a Colt .45 automatic, 1911 issue. Pop was a sergeant in Korea, brought her back with him. She's an old one, but I keep her cleaned and polished, and she works just fine." Philo handed the gun to Chance. "Here's ammo." He retrieved a leather pouch from another pocket and handed it over. "Thought you might want to carry her with you. You familiar with this sort of gun?"

Chance nodded. At his request, Maureen had taught him all about guns when she was with the NYPD. He'd wanted to know what it was like for her to carry a weapon.

"I've shot an automatic many times, Philo."

"She's accurate. No point in her sitting in my drawer when you might be needing her. This is a nasty situation and there's no telling what might happen."

Chance thought of refusing the gun, and then thought better of it. He wasn't about to underestimate Nevil. From what little Maureen had told him, the man was sly, diabolically clever, sociopathic. Chance was going to be prepared to take him on, should he be fortunate enough to have the opportunity.

"Thanks, Philo. I very much appreciate it."

"This whole thing is awful, just awful," Philo said, shaking his head. His salt-and-pepper hair was thinning on top, and he had it carefully combed to conceal the bald spot. "The wife and I both feel better, Chance, knowing you're here to take care of Maureen. She's our shirttail cousin, you understand. In fact, *everybody's* relieved you're here. And I know I'll relax a bit more now, knowing you got a little protection on you. These are bad people, whoever they are, taking sweet little girls away like that. Anything else I can do, you just say the word."

"It helps just to know all of you are supportive."

Philo nodded. "Sure thing." He squared his shoulders and cleared his throat, embarrassed but determined. "I want you to know as well that I may be getting older, but I still can hold my own in a fight. You just call on me if you figure you're heading into a tight situation. And oh, yeah, I nearly forgot. Howard Monroe—Howard's a reading consultant over at the school—well, anyhow, Howard's organizing search parties. One went out this afternoon, and there'll be more by tomorrow morning. Nothing that'll attract attention, you understand, just neighbors out two by two for walks. They'll be taking a careful look at every abandoned building anyone knows about. Howard's drawing up maps of the surrounding area, and we're planning to check abandoned buildings, sheds, old trailers—anyplace at all we figure somebody might be hiding. There's a lot of fathers and grandfathers around who're pretty upset about this."

Chance's heart swelled with gratitude. Living in the city, he'd seldom encountered the kind of universal concern and real caring these village people exhibited.

It made him feel grateful and humble, knowing there were still people like the ones in Cooper's Corner.

"You've heard about the gray van Trevor spotted this morning?" Philo asked.

Chance nodded. Obviously, there were no secrets possible in this village.

"Wanted Maureen and you to know we're all on the lookout for it. We're flagging down anything remotely suspicious and handing out pamphlets inviting folks to an autumn celebration on the village green. No such thing, but we'll deal with that when the time comes. Doc Dorn printed up a bunch of flyers on his computer this afternoon, and while we're handing them to the drivers, we'll take a good careful look in their van. So far we stopped two gray vans, but they were all damned leaf-peepers."

A lump formed in Chance's throat. He reached out a hand and shook Philo's, trying with the gesture to convey the gratitude he felt for the valiant efforts being made by the kind residents of Cooper's Corner. They at least were taking action, while he felt totally useless.

Philo returned the handshake, and the men touched each other's shoulders with closed fists. Philo left soon afterward, and Chance put the gun and ammo in the pocket of his leather jacket.

He found Maureen in the huge living room, pacing back and forth and glancing at her wristwatch every few moments. She turned toward him, and her face was frantic.

"He hasn't called. Why hasn't he called? It's almost

seven. I can't bear this waiting.'' The tension in her voice was palpable. "It's been ten hours, Chance. The girls need their supper and a bath, and I always read them a story before they go to sleep. They like a snack, they have cereal and milk—and—and I'm so scared that they're hungry and cold. I'm so afraid they're being mistreated. They'll—they'll be crying for me, I know they will.''

Her voice broke and she put both hands up to cover her face. Her entire body trembled violently, and a wild keening sound came pouring out of her. It went straight to Chance's heart. He could count on one hand the number of times he'd ever seen her cry.

In two strides he had her in his arms, held close against his chest. He was still wearing the shirt he'd put on that morning, and he could feel her wild tears soaking through it. Holding her for the first time in years, he was shocked by the fragility of her body. She'd always felt reed slender and incredibly strong, all smooth silky skin stretched taut over finely toned muscle.

Today, that strength was still there, but she'd grown dangerously thin. Every rib was evident beneath his stroking, soothing hands, and the deep inner trembling grew more pronounced instead of less as agony and the panic she'd been holding at bay finally ripped through her.

When the storm of tears slowed, she pulled away, searching through the pockets of her denim shorts for a tissue and not finding one.

Chance drew a handkerchief from his pants pocket and handed it to her.

She mopped her face and then looked up at him from swollen, miserable eyes. "You're the only man I've ever known who carries a real handkerchief," she sniffed. He smiled, and she added, "No matter what happened between us in the past, I'm glad you're here today, Chance." Her voice trembled.

A rush of warmth flooded through him, and he was about to answer when a tap came on the open door.

It was Harry Joyce, looking apologetic. "Sorry to intrude, but I wondered if Lydia and I could perhaps heat up some of those casseroles and interest you two in dinner?"

Maureen blew her nose and turned her attention to her guest.

"Harry, I'm so sorry about all this. Are you sure you and Lydia don't want to go to another B and B? I could give you numbers to call. There are several that I'd recommend—"

Harry shook his head and insisted it was something he and Lydia absolutely didn't want to do. "We'd rather stay here," he insisted. "We're retired, we don't have anywhere we have to go. We've got grandkids of our own about the age of your twins. Let us stay and help, please. It'll make us feel so much better to think we can help even a little."

"That's very kind, but you're not getting the attention you deserve," Maureen objected.

"You're not to even think about us," Harry insisted. "We're very independent. That is, unless it's too much of a bother for you, having us around?"

Maureen shook her head. "Not at all. You've been so supportive all day. But the truth is, I'm far too distracted and worried to be a hostess, Harry."

"We don't expect a thing," he assured her again. "We just want to help any way we can." He hesitated and then added, "Lydia and I ran a catering business for years. Food is our specialty. Why not let us manage the kitchen for the next few days? The food is piling up, and it needs to be stored properly. We'd feel as if we were being helpful if you let us take over that little chore."

"It would be a big relief," Maureen said. "I don't know what to do with all that stuff."

"We'd be delighted," he said with a smile. "And right now you should try to eat something, my dear."

Maureen shook her head. "I have no appetite at all, thanks, Harry. You and Lydia go ahead and eat."

"Oh, we didn't intend to suggest that you should feed *us* dinner." Harry sounded horrified. "We were only thinking of preparing a nice hot dinner for the two of you and then going out somewhere ourselves. B and B doesn't include dinner, we're aware of that."

"Harry, there's enough food in that kitchen to feed half of New York City, and most of it's going to go bad unless someone eats it," Maureen insisted. "It would be a favor to me if you and Lydia would have it."

"Well, thank you, Maureen, that's very kind. Will you join us?"

She shook her head. "Perhaps a little later, but not just now, thanks."

Harry hesitated, then nodded and left.

Maureen blew out a breath. "It's such an effort to be polite. I just want to scream at everyone, I feel so— so *angry.*"

"You're doing really well, Reen."

Her eyes welled up again with tears. "Chance, you go and have something to eat."

He shook his head. "I'll eat when you do." He sat down on one of the antique overstuffed sofas and patted the space beside him.

"Right now, I'd like you to sit down here and fill me in completely on Nevil. I want to know exactly what we're dealing with. You said earlier that there'd been attempts on your life since you moved here. Tell me about them, Reen."

She sank down on the sofa beside him, her hands clasping her long, bare legs. She was wearing shorts, and he noticed grass stains and dirt on her knees. There was garden soil under her fingernails. She was oblivious to the fact that evening was approaching and the September day had grown chilly as the sun disappeared. Her arms, too, were bare, and he could see goose bumps on them.

Tenderness overwhelmed him. She'd always been so independent, so self-sufficient. For the first time ever, she needed to be cared for. He wanted to reach over and draw her close to him, hold her, warm her against his body, but he wasn't sure how she'd respond.

There was so much anger between them still, buried

beneath this mutual concern for their children. They needed to clear it away, but right now, hearing about Nevil was more urgent.

He unfolded a knitted afghan and draped it around her shoulders.

He had to distract her, get her talking, take her mind away from the silence of the telephone and the fact that the day was almost over with no further word about the girls.

"How did it all start, Reen? I need to know the whole story."

She nodded and sighed. "I guess the beginning was that letter Frank got. It was addressed to me, to Maureen Maguire, care of NYPD, no return address. We'd just had our official opening when Frank phoned me about it. He read it to me."

She shivered, and Chance knew it wasn't from being cold.

"What did it say, Reen?"

"It was short, just two lines long. It wasn't signed, but I knew who it was from."

"Nevil." The word was like a curse on his lips.

She nodded. "It said, 'You can't hide from me. I will find you.'" She drew in a shuddering breath and released it. "That was the beginning of a terrible time for me, Chance."

If only he could promise her it was almost over.

CHAPTER SEVEN

"FRANK SENT THE LETTER TO forensics," Maureen said, "to see if Nevil's prints were on it, but there was nothing. We both figured there was no way Nevil could know I'd moved to Massachusetts, or that I was using my maiden name. Even so, after that I kept a close eye on every unknown guest who stayed here at the B and B. I even sent a glass to forensics with the prints of a guy who couldn't be identified, and it scored a hit. He was registered under a phony name—turned out he was a private investigator from New York."

"Who was he working for?"

"There was no way of telling. I had no proof that he was working for the Nevils, but I assumed my cover was blown."

"When did that happen?"

"Late last fall." Maureen laced her fingers tighter around her knees, her shoulders hunched. "I was on guard after that, but nothing else happened until early November. Then it got very cold almost overnight, and I loaned my coat to a guest staying at the B and B— Dr. Dorn's granddaughter, Emma. She was going for a walk with another guest, Blake Weston, who was also staying here. I gave her the sage-green coat and burnt-orange scarf I often wore. Emma's tall, with red highlights in her hair, and from a distance she could have been mistaken for me. Especially wearing my favorite coat.'' She drew in a shuddering breath. ''Someone shot at her, Chance.''

He made a shocked sound in his throat. ''Was she injured?''

Maureen shook her head. ''She wasn't, but Blake was. The bullet hit him in the side. Emma heard someone moving close by and she screamed for help, but whoever it was didn't respond. She got a really bad feeling, she felt as if they were in even more danger. They kept quiet. Blake was bleeding badly, and it was dark and raining and really cold. They somehow managed to make their way to a lean-to, where they sheltered for hours, until the Cooper's Corner volunteer rescue squad finally located them. It was just luck they were found in time. Blake was laid up for a while but he recovered fully. It could have been fatal for them both, though.''

''What did the police come up with?''

Maureen shrugged and shook her head. ''The bullet was from a shotgun. The police decided it was a hunting accident, but no hunter ever came forward, and whoever did the shooting was never found. There was absolutely nothing to go on.''

''You figure it was Nevil.'' It wasn't a question.

''I wasn't absolutely sure then. Now I am.''

''And that was the only attempt on your life?''

Maureen shook her head and made a harsh sound intended to be a laugh.

"Not by a long shot. The next thing that happened might not have been an attempt on my life, but it was very unsettling. I was putting a sign on one of the horse drawn sleighs for the Christmas Eve parade. I thought a car backfired, and the horses took off with my friend Grace and her daughter in the sleigh. Fortunately, no one was hurt. But I searched the area afterward and found a spent rifle shell. The noise that scared the horse was probably a gunshot. Again, no one saw anything, and there was no real proof to link the rifle shot to Owen."

Chance was feeling as horrified and frustrated as Maureen must have felt. "Do any of the local police know of your background with the NYPD?"

"Only Scott Hunter, the state trooper you met today."

"Were there any other incidents?" Chance was almost afraid to know.

Maureen sighed and nodded. "So many more, I can hardly keep them straight in my head. It seemed that those two were only the beginning."

She shivered, remembering, and drew her knees up against her chest. "I went out to the woodshed one evening last January, the way I always do, to bring in wood for the fireplace. When I opened the door and stepped inside, all of a sudden the roof caved in. All the logs came tumbling down and I was literally buried in wood. Thank goodness Clint heard the racket and came running. I got nailed pretty good with logs, and

I was so sore for a few days, I could hardly get out of bed. I was bruised from top to bottom."

Chance thought of the gun Philo had given him and was grateful all over again. The man behind these "accidents" was vicious, ruthless and clever.

"You were lucky you didn't end up with broken bones." He felt rage building inside of him. "That wasn't an accident, either, was it?"

Maureen shook her head. "Nope. The beams holding up the woodshed had been weakened. At first I thought it might have been animals, but after everything else that happened, I was convinced it was Owen Nevil who was responsible."

"I can't believe that the police would go on believing these things were accidental."

"Scott Hunter didn't think they were. He knew about the Nevil brothers and my background. But there was never any concrete proof—no clues that would lead to Owen Nevil."

"What happened next?" Chance was almost afraid to ask.

"Something that proved to me once and for all that Owen Nevil had found me. I went to check the rooms after a party we'd had and found a young woman unconscious in one of the beds. There was an empty pill bottle and we figured she'd taken an overdose. Luckily she came to and threw up, so she didn't need her stomach pumped. Dr. Dorn checked her out, and when she could talk, she said she was hitchhiking to New York and a guy named Owen picked her up. He offered her some coffee from a thermos, and she started getting groggy. He must have dropped her at the front door of Twin Oaks, and because of the party going on, no one noticed her sneaking into one of the rooms.''

"Do you think she was telling the truth? Did the police question her?''

Maureen nodded. "Scott grilled her, but her story hung together. He put out a warrant for Nevil, for questioning in Trudi Karr's doping. He wanted to hang an attempted murder charge on Nevil for it, but he's never been located.''

"Is this Karr woman still around?''

"Yeah, she's just a kid, really, only eighteen years old. Tom Christen, the Episcopal priest, got Burt and Lori Tubb to hire her as a waitress in their café. They also gave her a room in their house. Burt and Lori's kids are all grown, and they're lonely. They're very fond of Trudi, and she's blossomed since she came here.''

It was tough to listen to the things that had happened to Maureen. Chance knew it was probably ridiculous, but he felt that if he'd been around, he could have protected her.

"After that," she went on, "Clint and I were doubly cautious, but it wasn't enough. The next so-called accident still ties my stomach in knots.''

Maureen turned and looked at Chance, her green eyes weary. "There's an old well at the back of the property that had been boarded up to keep kids and animals from falling in. One day I noticed that some boards were missing. It was dangerous, doubly so because of the twins. I went and brought new boards and

was about to hammer them on when someone pushed
me from behind, really hard. Luckily, the well had
been half filled with dirt, but it was still too deep to
climb out of, and it was freezing cold down there.
After a while that seemed like a lifetime, my neighbor
came by and heard me hollering, but it was a really
scary experience. I knew it was Nevil who pushed me
in, even though I didn't see him. After that I started
carrying a gun again.''

Chance was silent, his face grim. He waited and
Maureen told him the rest of it.

''I was driving on one of the narrow mountain roads
and a truck forced me off to the side. My car flipped
and ended up in a muddy sinkhole. I was trapped inside and I barely made it out before it sank.'' She
slumped back in her chair, eyes closed.

Looking at her now, Chance studied the graceful
line of her throat, the high cheekbones, the sensuous,
full-lipped mouth. Her chestnut hair tangled and
pooled on the blue fabric of the sofa, and he longed
to reach out and touch it, refresh the memory of its
soft silkiness. Maureen had never been aware of how
lovely she was. He'd met other women, some more
beautiful, some less. All had paled in comparison to
her, not just her looks, but her spirit, her energy, her
passion.

How the hell had he managed to lose her? He'd
asked himself that so many times in the past couple
of years, and he'd never managed to come up with an
answer that satisfied him.

She began to talk again. ''There've been so many

incidents I actually began to wonder if maybe I was just paranoid, suspecting everyone and everything.'' She was quiet again, and then in a soft, sad voice she said, ''But then people started dying.''

Chance unclenched his hands, aware that he'd knotted them into fists. He was aching to drive them into Nevil's face. This urge to physically hurt another man was new to him. He'd played contact sports in college, he'd had his share of barroom brawls as a cocky young teenager, but he'd never felt this overwhelming desire to physically destroy another person.

He'd thought about physical violence sometimes, wondering if it was true that given the right circumstances, everyone had the capacity for murder.

At this moment, he didn't doubt it.

''Excuse me?'' A tap on the door drew his attention and Maureen's. It was Lydia Joyce with a tray holding fresh-made bread buns stuffed with ham and cheese, and two mugs of hot, strong coffee.

''We're determined to tempt you,'' she said, smiling at Maureen. ''Please do try and nibble on these buns.'' She set the tray on a small round table and drew it closer to Maureen, then, waving aside their thanks, hurried out. Chance handed Maureen one of the mugs and a roll.

She straightened her legs and accepted the drink and the food.

''It's become their mission not to let you starve,'' he told her with a smile.

''They're such nice people. I never met them before today and they already act like family. That's the thing about Twin Oaks—we attract such wonderful guests. We've had so many weddings here, for people who met and fell in love while they were visiting.''

He didn't comment, but he did wonder how many male guests had fallen in love with their beautiful, vibrant hostess. The thought sent a jolt of pure jealousy through his veins.

Maureen sipped at the coffee, but Chance noted that she placed the bun back on the tray.

He picked up his own cup, his mind involved again in Maureen's account of the horrors she'd endured during the past few months.

"Who died, Reen, and how?"

"It happened last spring. We hosted a birthday party, and someone left a box of chocolates in the rocking chair on the porch with a card that read, 'Thanks for being a great hostess.' I love chocolate— you remember that.''

He did. He'd been in the habit of buying her the finest imported chocolates to commemorate the day they met, the first time they'd made love, their wedding anniversary. Since their divorce, he'd never gone near the specialty shop where he'd purchased them on a regular basis.

"I almost opened them, but I wanted to fit in my swimsuit come summer, so I gave the box to a neighbor." Her voice faltered. "His name was Ed Taylor. He was such a sweet, gentle man. We used to buy chickens from him, and we didn't realize how nearly destitute he was until after he was gone. Poor, poor Ed. When I went to see him some time after that, I found him sprawled on the floor, dead. The box of chocolates was open, with several pieces missing. Toxicology reports could find nothing in the candy. The official cause of death was heart attack, but of course there are poisons that don't show up on toxicology screens. I know that Owen Nevil intended me to eat those chocolates and die. Ed ate them instead. I still feel responsible for his death.''

All Chance could feel was profound and selfish relief that Maureen hadn't been the one to eat the chocolates. And he instinctively knew that Ed Taylor wasn't the last of the victims, either.

''Who else died, Reen?''

Her hands were trembling and she put the cup back on the tray. When she looked at him, her green eyes were huge and profoundly sad.

''Dan,'' she whispered. ''My dear partner, Dan D'Angelo.''

''Dan's dead?'' Chance had known Dan well. He and Maureen had been invited to the D'Angelo home for barbecues and Christmas parties. It was a profound shock to hear that the big, jovial detective was gone. ''How?''

Tears gathered in Maureen's eyes and trickled down her cheeks. She brushed at them with the back of her hand. ''He'd retired from the NYPD and he and Mimi moved to Florida. He was out golfing—they said it was a freak accident. Someone hit him with a ball in the back of the head when he was poised for a putt. But there were no witnesses, and no one ever came forward. There's no question in my mind that Dan was murdered.''

Chance nodded agreement. ''First the informer and then your partner. That only leaves you, Reen.''

''Or my kids.'' There was panic in her tone. ''I tried to be so careful, Chance. I thought I was taking every precaution, but it wasn't enough.''

''It's not your fault.'' The words were vehement. Chance knew that she was blaming herself. ''It's not your fault, it's not Keegan's fault. Some things are not preventable.''

''Owen Nevil is both evil and very clever, a lethal combination,'' she said. ''I'll do whatever he asks, Chance. Anything. And you have to help me.'' She reached out a hand and put it on his arm. He covered it with his.

''You know I will. We're in this together.''

She nodded. ''But you have to give me your word that if it comes to a choice between my life and the girls, you'll take the twins and run.''

He shook his head. ''That's a choice I'm not sure I could make, Reen. You can't ask that of me, it's not fair.''

''None of this is fair.'' She grasped his hand, her fingers tightening, the urgency she felt evident in the pressure she exerted. Her voice rose.

''You *have* to, Chance. I know you. I know once you give your word, you'll stand by it. You have to promise me you'll do this for me. Please, please, Chance, give me your word.''

He could see how much stress Maureen had been

under this past year, and now she had to deal with the twins' kidnapping. She'd lost weight, and her velvety skin was drawn taut over her high cheekbones. There were dark bruises under her jade-green eyes, and every couple of minutes she glanced at the silent telephone.

She was close to breaking, he knew it. Maureen was one of the strongest women he'd ever known, both physically and mentally, but he knew all too well that everyone had a breaking point, and Maureen was dangerously close to hers.

Pity and something else, something he wasn't quite ready to admit to, made his chest ache. The need to protect her was overwhelming. The only thing he could do at this moment was try to set her mind at ease in any way possible. It would be the first time in his life that he gave his word with no intention of keeping the promise he made.

"I'll do what you ask," he finally said in a reluctant tone. It was all he could do to force the lie past his lips. "I promise you I'll put our children's lives first."

He hadn't prayed in a long time, but the words his mind formed now were sincere and desperate.

Don't make me choose, God. Please don't make me choose.

He groaned and reached out for her, and she came into his arms, pressing against him, wrapping her hands around his middle. She was trembling violently.

"Chance, oh God, Chance, what will I do. How can I go on living if—if—Nevil...?"

There was no need to complete the sentence. He knew exactly what she meant.

"Don't think about it." His voice was harsh. "It won't happen. We'll get them back."

Chance couldn't remember ever feeling stark terror. He thrived on stressful business deals, situations that pushed him to the limit. Physically, he played handball and ran and worked out at the company gym. He coached a basketball team at a boys' detention center, and he deliberately chose the most aggressive and angry young men to befriend. He enjoyed challenge, and normally met it head on.

But right now, he felt utterly helpless. He was all too aware that no demands for money had come from the kidnappers. It made his blood run cold to admit it, but he suspected it was because Nevil planned to murder Maureen, and perhaps the twins, as well. Too many attempts had already been made on her life. The awful truth was that Nevil wanted her dead.

He held her close, folding her against his body, trying to give her some of his own strength, mortally afraid that if their babies weren't found, this woman would withdraw, far beyond anyone's reach.

When her sobs quieted a little, he bent his head and took a risk. He lowered his head and gently kissed her, tasting the salt of her tears, and beneath it the uniquely sweet, achingly familiar essence that was, and always would be, Maureen.

And in that single moment he admitted what he'd fought against for almost five years—this was the only woman he'd ever loved. He'd never stopped loving her, despite the pain and anguish their divorce had caused him, despite the bitterness, the seething anger, the feeling of betrayal.

He couldn't lose her again. There was unfinished business between them.

The clock on the wall read five past nine.

Chance was reasonably certain now that Nevil wouldn't phone till morning. Those long, dark hours ahead were going to be torture for Maureen, and for him.

He knew how he longed to spend them, but making love to her just now wasn't an option.

So they'd talk.

CHAPTER EIGHT

CHANCE KEPT HIS TONE GENTLE, without accusation. "Reen, I need to know why you didn't tell me you were pregnant when we separated." He'd been furious about it earlier. Now he simply wanted to know.

She went very still in his arms.

"I tried." She sighed deeply, and her voice was devoid of passion, as if she'd spent all the available emotion she had. "I called your office four times, and three times Stacey told me you were too busy to talk to me. The fourth time, she said you'd gone to Paris and she didn't have a number where you could be reached. I decided if you were that busy and that determined to avoid me, you wouldn't have time to be a father, either. I never called again."

They had so much in common, he thought ruefully, and a great many of their similarities weren't positive ones. They were both stubborn, both had hair-trigger tempers, although they showed their anger in different ways. Neither could back down from an argument gracefully. And then there was pride. They each had more than their share, making it difficult to apologize.

"I was furious with you for not moving to France with me," he admitted. "And I was hurt. I actually thought you'd be excited about spending time in Europe.''

A year into their marriage, his business required him to relocate to Paris for at least a year. He'd mistakenly assumed Maureen would be glad to quit her job with the NYPD and come with him. He'd envisioned the two of them touring Spain, spending time in Greece, visiting Italy.

''It was arrogant and selfish of me to expect you to leave your job and just follow me,'' he admitted now.

''I didn't think you *had* to go to France,'' she confessed. ''I thought you could have stayed in New York and still had a job, while for me there was nothing in Paris comparable to what I had in New York. I went to college all those years, majored in criminal law, worked my butt off to make detective sergeant. I couldn't just walk away. I tried to tell you that.''

She *had* told him so, repeatedly. All he'd heard her saying was that she didn't care enough about him to come with him. The quarrels had escalated, and after one particularly bad fight, she'd packed and moved out, into an attic apartment he'd only seen once. He'd gone there in the middle of the night to beg her to come home, and she'd called the cops on him.

He'd left for Paris two full weeks before he'd planned on going, and Maureen immediately filed for divorce. He was served with the papers one morning while he was chairing a meeting in a Paris boardroom. He'd fired two supervisors that day, knowing he was being grossly unfair and not giving a damn. That night he'd gotten drunker than he'd ever been, and picked a street fight with some thugs. He'd fought like a madman, and he'd won when he wanted to lose, to be knocked senseless, to be in such physical pain he wouldn't feel the other.

"I was sick day and night, throwing up, dizzy," she murmured. "I thought I was just upset over our marriage ending. Then one day I fainted at work and Dan packed me into the car and took me to Emergency. The doctor there told me I was pregnant. I tried to call you that night, but you wouldn't even talk to me."

"I'm so sorry about that." He'd always thought regret was a useless emotion, but he couldn't stop it from rolling through him now. "It was just too painful to speak to you, Reen, and every time we did talk we went round and round the same old issues without any resolution, and I kept on losing my temper. I finally told Stacey to refuse any calls from you. God, I was such a fool. Can you ever forgive me?"

He longed to ask if she could ever love him again, but it wasn't the time or the place. And he was also afraid to ask, he admitted. He knew how it felt, living without Maureen in his life. He wasn't sure he could stand it if she said no and he had to go back to the kind of half life he'd had since their divorce.

"I'm not sure."

Her answer hurt.

"I can't really think about it right now, Chance. I can't think about anything except the girls."

At least she hadn't said a flat-out no. He had to be content with that for the moment.

The trembling in her body had quieted. She sat

within the circle of his arms for some time, but after a while she sighed deeply and moved away, and he felt bereft.

His arms, his heart, his life, all felt empty. He looked at her and vowed that he wouldn't let her out of his sight if he could help it, not until this was over. He'd do everything in his power to protect her. He longed to have his daughters safe, and the thought of the danger they were in brought him very near despair.

They were so small, so vulnerable. He was their daddy, and with every cell in his body he ached to protect them. Where were they? What the hell could he do to find them, bring them home where they belonged?

"BILLY, WE WANT TO GO HOME now, okay?" Randi could hardly keep her eyes open, but still she fought sleep.

"Please?" Robin echoed. "It's time for bed, Billy. We have to go home to bed, okay?"

Outside the curtains, the city was dark. Streetlights were on, and the usual bustle on the sidewalks far below had intensified.

Billy was worn out with trying to entertain the girls. He knew they were hungry and scared. Angie usually made some macaroni or something for supper, but she hadn't yet, and there was no telling when or even if she'd get around to it. He'd told her more than an hour ago that the girls couldn't sleep because they needed something to eat. She'd sworn at him and then said she'd fix something, but so far there was no sound coming from the kitchen.

Maybe she'd let him heat up a can of soup for them. He went out to ask her, but she was on the telephone, and he knew better than to interrupt her. He hovered just outside the bedroom doorway, and he shivered when he heard her say his brother's name.

"Yeah, well, Owen, don't think you're gonna dump them on me for very long. You said one day and one night. It's bad enough having an older kid around. What is it with you and kids, anyhow? You don't like 'em any more than I do. It pisses me off that you think you can just dump them here and I'll take care of them for you."

Billy shuddered. He hated and feared Owen. He wondered if Angie knew that he could hurt her if she got lippy with him that way.

"Yeah, I know you will, lover." Angie sounded a little happier. Billy figured Owen was promising her money or jewelry or something. Angie loved jewelry. Billy wondered how long it was going to be before Owen found out Angie was seeing that other guy, Rocky. He'd come home with her from the bar three times now.

Owen had been out of town those times, but he had a habit of turning up without telling anybody he was coming. Billy didn't want to be around when Owen found out. Too many times he'd seen Owen mad, and it scared him something awful. His half brother's eyes got red, and instead of hollering he got real quiet. Billy and his sister used to try to hide when Owen came home like that. Sometimes it worked, but all too often he found them. Billy didn't want to think about what happened then.

The twins were crying again. Billy sneaked into the kitchen and found a box of cheese crackers. He took the half-empty quart of milk out of the fridge and hurried back into the bedroom.

They were sitting in the middle of the bed, arms wrapped around each other, tears rolling down their cheeks, long eyelashes clumped together. It brought a lump to Billy's throat, seeing them like that. They were just babies. People oughta take care of babies. His sister had always taken care of him, as best she could.

He taught them how to drink out of the milk jug, and the novelty took their mind off things. He doled out the crackers and they munched them down.

When there was no more milk and the crackers were gone, Randi yawned, and like an echo, Robin did, as well. Billy took them to the bathroom, and when they were finished, he helped them back on the bed, brushed away the crumbs from the crackers and tucked them under the grimy comforter, plumping up the pillow under their heads.

"Can you tell us a story, Billy?"

The afternoon had been endless, and he'd read them all the stories he had. He'd soon realized they didn't mind hearing them over and over. But he was really tired of reading them again and again. He thought for a minute, and then he remembered a story his sister had told him when he was little.

"Once upon a time there was a prince and princess whose mommy and daddy loved them very much," he began. "They lived in a castle in a faraway land, where the trees were always filled with apples, and grapes and pomegranates grew everywhere."

"What's pomegrand?" Robin's voice was sleepy. Randi's eyes were closing.

"It's a round red thing, about this size." He cupped his hands. "It's like a ball, but when you cut it open it has all these little red seeds that taste sweet. And there's juice in it, too." His sister had bought him a pomegranate once. He could remember how he'd savored it, taking three days to dig out all the seeds.

"Can we have some pomegrand, Billy?"

"Sure." It wasn't right to lie to them, but he knew from experience that a little kid needed something sweet to dream about. "Maybe tomorrow we'll get one."

Her mouth quivered and she whispered, "We want to show Mommy the pomegrand, okay, Billy?"

"Sure. You can show it to your mommy." He didn't like to think about what would happen to them tomorrow, whether they'd get to be with their mommy or not. Owen was mean and hardly ever kept his word. Even if he'd promised to take them back to wherever they lived, Billy figured it was a lie. Owen never kept his promises or returned things he'd stolen.

They lay cuddled close in each other's arms as they fell asleep, and Billy felt a little envious. If you had a twin, you'd never really be alone, would you? But then he thought it over and decided that having a twin wouldn't be any different or better than having a sister. Owen would just find ways to keep them apart, the way he was doing now. Billy thought about his sister, and love and loneliness welled up inside him.

All he wanted in the world was the chance to live with her, just the two of them, far away from Owen. She was old enough now to take care of him until he grew big, and then he'd take care of both of them. He wished he'd grow older faster.

Owen had promised that if she did what he told her this one last time, he'd let them be together from now on, but Billy was scared to even hope that would come true.

He climbed up on the bed beside the twins and fought back the tears that threatened whenever he thought about his sister and Owen.

Where was she right now? He hoped she was okay. Sobs built, burning in his throat and chest, and finally, shoving his head under a corner of the comforter, he gave in to them. He couldn't help it. He hoped that Angie wouldn't hear. The television was still blaring, filling the small apartment with sound.

TWIN OAKS GREW SILENT as darkness fell and the temperature dropped.

Keegan had gone up to bed, hugging the puppy.

Chance figured there could be frost before morning. He lit a fire in the huge fireplace in the living room. A gigantic harvest moon turned the fields and trees outside the windows to eerie silver.

The phone was ominously silent, and when he and

Maureen ventured into the kitchen, they found it gleaming, counters empty, floor shining. The Joyces had cleaned up and somehow stowed away the massive quantities of food, storing it all in the large fridge, the freezer and the old-fashioned pantry.

They'd also made a fresh pot of coffee and heated up a bowl of homemade chicken soup for Maureen and Chance before they went up to their room.

"The two of you have to eat to keep up your strength," Lydia insisted. "We're off to bed now, but we want you both to know we'll pray for your twins before we go to sleep."

Maureen had thanked them again but didn't touch the soup. As far as Chance could figure, she hadn't eaten anything all day, or rested, either. She seemed to burn with a frantic flame, her too-slender body restless, her eyes sunken and haunted.

"I doubt he'll call tonight, Reen," Chance said gently. "Why don't you come back into the living room and lie down on the sofa? Maybe try to sleep a little. I'll listen for the phone."

She shook her head. The dark circles under her beautiful green eyes were more pronounced.

"I couldn't sleep, Chance. All I can think about is the twenty-four-hour golden rule. In law enforcement, the first twenty-four hours in any crime are crucial. They represent the optimal opportunity to solve the crime. And I feel as if those precious hours are slipping past without my doing anything."

"But what more is there to do?" It was the question he'd been asking himself all day. "We've talked about it, and it seems we're doing absolutely everything we can, short of alerting the authorities."

Maureen nodded, her face a study in misery. "I know you think we ought to do that, Chance. I'm sorry I can't agree to it."

He did think it was the right thing, but he wasn't about to argue with her. He sighed and gave her a halfhearted smile.

"I'm not the one with the police background, Reen. You're the expert in that area. I wouldn't for a moment do anything that you thought might endanger our girls' lives."

He didn't add *further*. He didn't have to. Her eyes met his and they silently acknowledged that their daughters' lives were already in serious danger, but neither of them spoke the words aloud again.

CHAPTER NINE

IN THE LIVING ROOM HE ADDED wood to the fire and closed the wire grate on the bright, warm flames, then took her hand and led her to the sofa. When she was seated, he sat down beside her.

"Tell me about Randi and Robin. Tell me everything, from when you found out you were pregnant until they were born, from their birth until now." He wanted to distract her, but he also had a burning desire to know every last detail about his daughters.

"I told you I was sick." She attempted a smile, and it tore at his heart that he hadn't been there for her when she needed him. "For three months, it seems as if all I did was throw up. There'd be two hours in the afternoon when the sickness lifted, and then I was ravenously hungry. I'd eat everything that wasn't nailed down, and it felt so good—for all of two hours. Then I'd start vomiting again."

"I should have been there to help you." Regret was bitter in his throat.

"Yeah, you should have." The words weren't blaming. She was just acknowledging a simple fact.

"After a while, I got used to being sick. Isn't it weird, how you can get used to almost anything?" Her lips trembled, and he saw the effort she made to control herself.

"I never got used to being apart from you, Reen." The quiet words were out before he could stop them.

She looked at him and gave a shy little nod. "I know what you mean." A heartbeat later she added, "I guess I never got used to it, either."

In spite of everything, his heart soared. He reached over and took her hand in his. It seemed as if his very skin held the sensory memory of her, of the pliable long bones, the strength in her fingers and narrow wrists. He stroked a finger across her knuckles. Her hands were silent witnesses to how hard she'd worked here at Twin Oaks. Her skin was slightly rough, and there were calluses on her fingers, small scars from wounds that had healed.

He raised her hand and pressed his lips to her palm. She didn't pull away, but she didn't acknowledge the action, either.

"Then, at the end of the third month, I suddenly stopped being sick, as if some magic button had been pushed." She'd gone back to the story of her pregnancy, and he knew it was because it felt safer than exploring the breakdown of their relationship.

"I knew by then I was having twins," she said. "I'd had an ultrasound, and I couldn't believe it when the doctor laughed and said there were two. I should have expected it. There're so many twins in the Cooper family. Remember, we used to speculate about it?"

"I remember everything, Reen."

"I didn't want to know whether they were girls or

boys, though. I wanted it to be a surprise. All I cared about was that they'd be healthy.''

"I'd have felt exactly the same." He was eager for every slightest detail, every image of this precious time he'd missed.

"Then I started eating and I couldn't stop. I got absolutely monstrous." She shook her head and rolled her eyes. "I figured I'd have to wear tents for the rest of my life—I couldn't imagine ever being skinny again. My belly button popped out, and it felt like my skin was about to burst. At first, they rocketed around like hockey players, but as they grew larger they didn't move a whole lot. I guess there just wasn't room in there. Toward the end I could barely walk. I don't know how mothers do it when they carry more than twins. I was so huge I couldn't even drive, I didn't fit behind the wheel of a car. And I didn't dare go into a small bathroom for fear I'd get stuck on the throne."

He wished he could have seen her then, big with his babies. He knew he would have found her incredibly beautiful. He found her that way at this moment.

"They were big babies?" It was like a physical craving, this need to know everything about his daughters, about Maureen.

"Six pounds each, big for twins. Randi was a few ounces more, but their birth weights were very close."

"Tell me about when they were born." Terrible nostalgia overwhelmed him. She'd been in labor with his twins, and he hadn't even known.

"Clint took me to the hospital, and Dan came as soon as he heard." Her tiny smile was bittersweet.

"They were both so funny, trying to be strong and manly, and both of them so nervous, I wondered if they were going to make it through without passing out. My obstetrician wanted to do a caesarian, but I balked. I insisted she give me a chance to have them the old-fashioned way."

She was the bravest person he'd ever met, and he told her so now.

"You might not have thought so that night," she replied. "Nobody really tells you the truth about child-birth, you know. It's pretty extreme. I screamed the place down. But once I got into it, I got stubborn and decided there was no way I'd give in and ask for a caesarian unless the babies were in danger. And they weren't, but it was one of the longest nights of my life. Randi was born at 6:46 a.m., July 29, and Robin came along ten minutes later."

Her face lit up at the memory, her eyes sparkling for the first time since he'd arrived. He cherished this moment of happiness the memories brought her, even as he regretted the lost opportunity to welcome his daughters into the world.

"Oh, Chance, they were so funny-looking. I know all mothers are supposed to think their babies are beautiful, but I confess I laughed when I saw the poor little mites. I couldn't help it. They were blood streaked, and they had these bumpy pointed heads and such outraged little purple faces. They were shrieking away, and they had so much black hair—it was as dark as yours at first."

That pleased him. He could almost feel his chest expanding with pride.

"Their hair was absolutely wild, long enough for the nurses to pull up in goofy little ponytails on top of their heads. Eventually it all fell out, and they were bald as eggs for quite a while. I started to wonder if they'd ever get hair, and then it grew in again thick and the exact color of mine. The first thing I did after they were born was check them from top to bottom, to make sure they had everything they needed."

There was awe in her voice even now. "Their bottoms were smaller than the palm of my hand, and I could see they were going to have gorgeous long legs, and their toenails and fingernails were minute, but absolutely perfect. I couldn't believe how perfect they were, I kept taking their clothes off for the first few days just to look at them."

It was ridiculous, but tears welled up in his eyes as she described her first glimpse of their daughters.

"I nursed them all during my maternity leave from the NYPD. I had gallons of milk," she said with more than a touch of pride. "It was so exhausting, though. They didn't wake up at the same times, so I'd just finish feeding and changing one and the other would want to eat. When I look back on it, it seems as if all I did for three full months was feed and change babies. At night I could never remember which twin I'd just fed, and I'm sure sometimes one got fed twice and the other not at all."

"Didn't you have any help?" He'd insisted on a generous divorce settlement, but she'd instructed her lawyer to refuse it. He'd felt hurt all over again that she wouldn't accept his money, and any lingering urge he'd had to contact her was squelched. He'd isolated himself from her totally then.

What a complete jerk he'd been. He'd lost so much to arrogance and pride and plain old stubborn idiocy.

"I hired a woman to come in and cook and clean for me. I couldn't have done it otherwise. And once my leave was over, I had a nanny who cared for them. Her name was Nina. She was a sweet young Mexican woman with a baby of her own. She loved them and took wonderful care of all the babies. But I missed being with them full-time. Then after the trial that put away Carl Nevil, I began to rethink my future. Now that I had the girls, I took Carl's threat more seriously. When our great-uncle Warren Cooper willed Clint and me this property, it was like a gift from heaven. It was a chance for a new life for us and our kids. Kristin's death was horrible for Clint and Keegan, and I'd changed once the twins were born. My career wasn't my first priority anymore."

She shook her head. "Ironic, huh? We divorced over issues related to my career, and then I realized there were things far more important. I wanted the twins to be somewhere safe, where I could watch them grow. So Clint and I talked it over, and in the end we both quit our jobs, came out here and gradually turned the old farmhouse into this bed-and-breakfast."

"That took guts," Chance commented.

"It also took a ton of elbow grease. It's an old house, and it was pretty run-down when we started."

Chance glanced around at the warm and welcoming room. From what he'd seen of it, Twin Oaks looked rock solid and in good repair. "It's a beautiful house, Reen. When this is over, you'll have to give me a guided tour."

"I will. Clint and I are really proud of what we've accomplished. It ate up all our combined savings and a lot of hard labor, but it was a labor of love. We had lots of help. Cooper's Corner has an excellent plumber and a wonderful carpenter-electrician. And there were people eager to work as casual laborers."

Chance could tell by the way the rapid words poured out that she was using them to avoid thinking, and he was grateful she was able to do so.

"We got more advice from the locals than we really needed, a lot of it conflicting, but it felt good to have neighbors who cared enough to tell us how to do things. Clint restored the woodwork and refinished all the floors. I did the interior decorating, sewed all the curtains and quilt covers and pillows. I really enjoyed doing it."

"I remember how you decorated our apartment in New York, using those dramatic colors on the walls and finding bargains at flea markets that I thought were junk until you fixed them up."

He also remembered leaving that apartment for the last time. Even though she'd been gone several weeks, his ears still seemed to be ringing with the bitter accusations they'd thrown at each other. It had been a rainy, dark New York afternoon when he left, the darkest day he could remember living through. He'd sold the apartment furnished, naively believing he could leave all the memories behind that way. How stupid he'd been, what an utter fool.

Once he was in Europe, he'd begun dating a succession of beautiful women and found that he could barely remember their names. He'd lived in stylish apartments since, but none had ever felt as much like home as that modest little walk-up in the Village. But it wasn't the place, he realized now. *This* was home, sitting holding the hand of the woman he loved. Wherever Maureen was, that was where his life felt right.

"Tell me what our girls are like, now they're a little older," he begged. "What kind of personalities do they have?"

Maureen's smile was bittersweet, but it was a smile nonetheless. "Randi tends to be bossy. I told you she's the one like you."

"Me, bossy?" Chance playfully ruffled her hair with his hand.

Maureen nodded. "But she's also the most sensitive. Robin's thoughtful and the quieter of the two, but things don't bother her as much. Randi's the one with the temper—she can throw herself down and kick and scream with the best of them." For just a moment, she smiled again and managed even to tease. "She gets that from you, too, Chance. We both know I don't have a temper at all."

His eyebrow rose and he gave her a significant look, making her roll her eyes and smile.

"I seem to remember getting beaned with a book once when your temper got the best of you." He also

remembered vividly how that fight had gotten re-
solved, and by the way she shifted and avoided his
gaze, he knew she was remembering, as well. Sexual
awareness flared bright and hot for a moment, but
Chance knew it wasn't the time to act on it.

"Do they talk yet?" He drew the conversation back
to safer ground and tried to imagine how his daughters' voices sounded. "I've never been around little
kids much, you know. I have no idea when they start
talking." He'd been an only child, his parents older
when he was born, and with no relatives in New York,
he'd had a lonely childhood.

"Oh, you should hear them. They talk all the time,
and they argue. They have a sixth sense about each
other, and finish each other's sentences, and even
when they're not together, one knows when the other
is hurt." Once again, words tumbled out. "They
learned to walk on the same day, within an hour of
each other. I tried to put them in separate cribs when
they were about six months old, but they cried all
night. I finally had to push two cribs together and leave
the sides down so they could hold hands. If one gets
sick, the other does, too. They're very close."

Maureen's fingers tightened on his as a new, terri-
fying thought crossed her mind. "He wouldn't separate them, would he, Chance? I don't know if they'd
survive, alone and away from each other."

He didn't know. She knew that. What she needed
was mindless reassurance, and he gave it.

"Of course not. What would be the point? They're
together, Reen, don't imagine anything different." She

needed distraction again. "Tell me what they like to do, what they eat, how they play."

"They're so busy. And so funny. They wake up at six-thirty every morning, and they come into my room to wake me up. They climb on the bed and snuggle up to me, giggling and whispering in my ear. They—" Her voice trembled. "They kiss me awake, big sloppy kisses. They shower with me, they love apple shampoo and perfume and dusting powder—they're very feminine that way. We've had more than a few disasters, when they get into my stuff and spill it all over. And then we get dressed together. They always want to wear something similar to what I'm wearing, shorts or jeans, or even once in a great long while, a dress."

Chance smiled at that. He knew Maureen preferred easy, casual clothing. Every so often she would put on a short dress and stockings and heels, mischievously teasing him and turning him on. He used to feel so flattered, but of course clothing had nothing to do with the passion he felt for her.

"They're learning to get their clothes on right, but they still put things on backward now and then," she said. "And shoes are tough. They invariably get them on the wrong feet. But they've been toilet trained since they were two—they like being clean." She sounded breathless when she added, "Oh, Chance, they're the best little girls, the sweetest."

His heart started to hammer as she drew in a shuddering breath and then turned and buried her face against his shoulder. He could smell the apple shampoo on her hair, the unique scent of her skin, and a deep hunger stirred.

"We just *have* to get them back safe," she said in an anguished rush. "We just *have* to, Chance. I want you to know them, I want them to get to know their daddy."

It was the first definite indication he'd had that she might consider a future with him in it. His voice was choked when he said, "I want that, too, Reen. More than anything, I want that." It was time he told her the truth. "I love you, Reen. You're the only woman I've ever loved. And I love those little girls, even though I've never seen them. I want you, and I want them. I want us to be a family."

He stroked a palm down her silky mass of hair, and his heart gave a thump when she said with a half sob, "I want that, too."

And then she lifted her face up, wordlessly inviting him to kiss her.

CHAPTER TEN

THE FEEL OF HER LIPS, soft and eager, tasting of salt tears, fueled the raging desire that flared in him.

Her arms wrapped tighter around him, pulling him close. Her mouth was as ferociously hungry and greedy as his, touching and tasting.

She took his hand and pressed it on her breast, and if there was a sense of desperation to her passion, it was there in him, as well. He knew if he went slow, gave either of them time to think, the moment would be lost. Just for a few moments, he needed to break away from the tight, weary coils of worry and fear that bound the two of them. He wanted so much to take her with him, and it seemed that was what she wanted, too.

She was kissing him, pulling at his clothing and hers, all the while making a low sound in her throat, a steady moan of lost and frantic need that made him lose the last of his control.

He unfastened her shorts, she undid his belt. She was moving against him, harsh and urgent, even before their clothing was fully off. Her hand encircled him, guiding him as he entered her, and then he could no more have stopped what was happening than cease breathing.

She was slippery and hot and frenzied. He could feel himself starting to come as she convulsed and cried out, head thrown back, her long, slender, almost fragile body shuddering with the intensity of her climax.

With his last rational thought, he reached out and took her face in his hands, tipping her head toward him so he could look deep into her eyes as he poured himself into her.

When it was over, his body sagged against her. Her arms loosened their hold around his torso, her muscles boneless and spent. The sofa wasn't wide enough for them to lie comfortably, and after a few moments she gave a ragged sigh and sat up, reaching for her underwear, shirt and shorts and pulling them on.

As reason returned, he grew tense and anxious. Would she think he'd taken advantage at a time when she was most vulnerable? *Was* that what he'd done? It had happened so quickly, he hadn't had time to think it through. He hadn't wanted to think, he admitted miserably.

"It's still there, isn't it, Chance?" There was a dreamlike quality to her voice. She pushed her tousled hair back and turned to him, her face open and loving, raw with sated desire. She stroked a hand tenderly down his jaw. "In the midst all of this horror, we still have this fine thing, you and I. And for just these few moments, it's made it easier to breathe. All day, I've felt as if I couldn't breathe."

It was all right. His relief was overwhelming. He

should have known she was too honest to ever blame him for what they'd chosen to do together.

He told her what he was thinking, what he'd been afraid of. It was a thing he'd never been able to do before, confess his most intimate fears. Before, he would have considered it a weakness. Now he saw it only as a benefit of love. He'd changed in this single day, profound changes that he knew were lasting.

He sat up, put his trousers and shirt back on, and then massaged her shoulders. Even after their loving, the muscles were like rope, taut and hard and twisted into knots, and he worked on them gently and thoroughly. For a few moments, she almost relaxed.

She hadn't looked at the clock for a long while, but she did again now, and she gave a moan of despair, wrenching herself away from him and springing to her feet.

"Oh, God, Chance, it's after 1:00 a.m. Randi and Robin have been gone sixteen hours. I know there's nothing we can do until the phone call comes, but this is torture for me." She paced across the large room and back again, the renewed anguish she felt evident on her face.

All he could think of was to get her to talk to him again.

"Give me a crash course in Randi and Robin," he suggested. "There's still so much about them I don't know. What do they like to eat for breakfast, for instance?"

As it had before, talking about the girls took the edge off her panic.

"Eggs, and toast if I cut off the crusts. I make them porridge. They'll eat it if I put maple syrup on it. They love Clint's chocolate chip cookies—they're a big treat. But mostly they have fruit and raw veggies for snacks. They like carrots, and they love raw broccoli."

"Broccoli?" He pulled a face, hoping to make her smile even a little, and his heart skipped a beat when he was rewarded. "I can't believe any kids of mine would love broccoli."

"They call it night flower. They got it out of a book I used to read them."

"What books do they like?"

"They had one they needed to hear every night for over a year called *Where the Wild Things Are*. And now they're insatiable. There's no one special book, they just want me to read one after the other. They love a goofy one Clint found for them called *The Adventures of Captain Underpants*."

"What about music? Do they like music?" One of the things he and Maureen had shared was a love of music. They'd gone to concerts in the park, the symphony, Broadway musicals.

"Is it an inherited trait, the love of music, Reen?"

Again, a nostalgic smile came and went. "It must be, because they love music. They ask me to turn on the CD player, and they dance. They like rock and roll. They're so funny, they wriggle their little bottoms and wave their arms and really get into it. They started to sing before they could talk, and both of them can carry a tune even without knowing the words."

Wanting to know them, have them know him, was so overwhelming it made his chest ache.

"You mentioned it was likely Nevil had an accomplice here in the village. Is there anyone you can think of who might be connected to him?"

She blew out a frustrated breath, but he could see that once again, her mind was occupied. She grew calmer, and after a few moments once again sank down on the sofa beside him, tucking her legs under her tailor fashion, resting her arms on her knees and gazing into the fire.

"I've racked my brains trying to think who it could be. I've made lists of all the villagers, how long they've been here, what I know of their backgrounds, who their relatives are. And I've kept careful tabs on any newcomers, as well."

"Show me your notes. Maybe together we'll see something that you missed."

She got up and went into the office across the hall, coming back in a few moments with a notebook.

"These are the longtime residents—it's not likely it would be any of them," she explained, pointing to a list on the right-hand side of a page.

She indicated the list on the left. "These are newcomers, people who've arrived since Clint and I got here almost two years ago and who don't seem to have any real connection to the town. Some of them are already gone. They were transients who worked for the summer in the orchards."

She flipped a page, indicating half a dozen names. "These are the ones who are still around, and this is what I know about them, what jobs they're doing. I don't have a lot of background on most of them, so I sent their names to Frank. He was only able to trace these two. The others didn't show up on the system, and the department doesn't have the means to put any manpower on something as nebulous as this.''

She pointed to two names underlined with red pen. ''Jon Durham has a juvenile record for possession, two counts, suspended sentence. He's twenty-two now and seems to have straightened out. He's working for Seth Castleman, the local carpenter-electrician. Seth seems to think he's an okay guy, but Durham doesn't reveal much about himself.''

''You've met him? What did you think of him?''

''Reserved. He's certainly polite. He lives in an old trailer in a deserted orchard just out of town. Keeps to himself. Scott Hunter hasn't had any complaints about him. He's got a dog he cares a lot about named Sheba. He doesn't have much money but he called Alex McAlester when she had puppies and ran into trouble delivering. That's where Satin came from. Jon was looking for homes for them and he came by and asked if the twins would like one of them. Of course they fell in love the first time they laid eyes on Satin. He brought the puppy over several times to let them get used to her, but Satin was too little to be away from her mother until just a couple of days ago.''

''So he's familiar with the back yard? He'd have seen the shed and the lock on the door?''

Maureen nodded. ''He was in the back yard several

times, and he was out there for an hour the other day, the day he brought Satin over.''

''Maybe we should try to find out where he was yesterday morning.''

Maureen agreed. ''I'll see if he was at work with Seth. I'll call him in another few hours—Seth's always up early.''

Chance glanced at the notebook again, at the second name. ''What did you find out about this Edward Gaton?''

''He has a French accent and he claims to be writing a book. He's renting a cottage from Gavin Cornwall, one of the local old-timers. Frank got a hit on Gaton. He was arrested at a riot in Boston two years ago, charged with assaulting a police officer. He's forty-four and had no priors before the riot. He's been here most of the summer, a surly man who keeps to himself except for frequent visits to the library. I've seen him around the village but never spoken to him. Beth, the woman that Clint married, is the local librarian, and she knows him better than anyone. She's the one who gave me the few facts I have on him. He told her he grew up in France, in a small village near the border of Spain, but that's all he'd tell her. As far as I know, he hasn't been around Twin Oaks or the babies at all, but Beth said he was really interested in the Cooper history. He's read everything the library has on our family, which seems weird to me. If he's that interested, why hasn't he ever come to the house or even introduced himself to either Clint or me?''

''Did Beth ask him what his book's about?''

Maureen nodded. "All he'd say was that it was related to the American men who fought in France during the Second World War."

Chance nodded and flicked back to the list of people that Frank hadn't been able to find out about. "Are there any more on here you have reason to be suspicious of, Reen?"

"I've had to be suspicious of everyone," Maureen said with a sad shake of her head. "I hate feeling that way. You saw today how kind and loving most of the villagers are. But I can't afford to trust anyone too much, because there simply has to be a spy in the village. Nevil's known my every move."

She gestured at the names. "There are two women I've been curious about. One is Zaire Haddock. She arrived in town just three weeks ago, so it's unlikely she'd have had anything to do with the incidents last winter. She's young, maybe twenty, twenty-two. She got a job at the gift shop, but apparently she asks lots of questions about everyone, including me. Edna and Mary don't know much about her, and all she's said is that her mother died a year ago. I wouldn't be concerned about her except that she's paid a lot of attention to the twins. She dropped by a week ago and asked a zillion questions about them. I notified Frank, but he couldn't get a trace on her."

"Red-haired girl?"

Maureen nodded. "This week, anyhow. She's changed her hair color twice since she arrived."

"I think I saw her when I was mailing the bolt cutters. She really gave me the once-over." He remembered the young woman's penetrating look. Working in the gift shop, she'd be sure to know all about the kidnapping. She'd also know who he was by now, and that word had spread around town despite Maureen's warnings.

"Who's the other woman?"

"Trudi Karr."

Chance nodded, remembering what Maureen had told him. "That's the young woman who had the run-in with Owen Nevil, the one he drugged."

"Yes. Dr. Dorn figures she's had a hard life. She has no self-esteem, and she's jumpy, like a girl who's been brutalized. The Tubbs have sort of adopted her. Most of their kids and grandkids live out of state and they miss them, so Trudi fills a gap. She seems really grateful to them for everything, and she's caught on pretty well to waitressing in their café. I've heard that at first she was a disaster, but Lori was really patient with her. I asked Lori if she talks about her childhood, says anything at all about where she's from, but she doesn't. I've talked to her, and she's not open at all about her background. In spite of my suspicions, I like the girl. I feel sorry for her, but I've just never been sure about that story she told, about Owen Nevil drugging her."

"But if she was the informant, wouldn't you think she'd have kept quiet about Nevil?"

"It depends how clever she is. It's a good way to make herself seem innocent. But she's also the only person in the village who's actually admitted talking to him."

"Frank didn't get anything on her?"

Maureen shook her head. "Not a thing. The last address she gave was a house in New York that's been torn down, and nobody in the neighborhood seems to remember her."

He wanted to go out right now, pull each and every one on the list out of bed, force them somehow to tell what they knew—if, indeed, they knew anything at all. "So it could be any one of these people."

"Or none of them. Chance, I feel so frustrated, because there's really nothing to go on." Her voice dropped to a whisper. "What are we going to do?"

He slid an arm around her and drew her close.

"We're going to face this together, and we're going to get the girls back safely. You're not alone, Reen. I'm here with you, and when this is over, we'll talk about our future as a family."

He held his breath, waiting for what she would say. It was a long time coming.

"I want that, Chance. You must know how much I want you, judging by what just happened between us. But we've got a lot of catching up to do, a lot of changing, both of us." Her voice grew wistful. "Do you think it could work for us? We're still the same people. We couldn't make it work before, even though the sex was fantastic. It still is, but sex won't..."

Chance put a finger on her lips, shushing her. He followed it with a kiss, a gentle reaffirmation of the fact that he loved her.

"I don't know about you, but I'm not the same person anymore," he murmured in her ear. "I've learned what's really important to me, and believe me, Reen, it's not the business. I enjoy my job, but I want you and the girls more than anything else. When this is over, we can figure out what's best for all of us, how best to create a life that's right for the four of us."

If only they got the girls back safely. He didn't dare contemplate what life would be like without them, for him or for Maureen.

She'd closed her eyes when he kissed her. She opened them now and looked at him, tired and uncertain, wary. "I'm so frightened, Chance. For the girls, and for—for me." Her voice was low, husky. "I couldn't stand losing them, but I couldn't stand losing you again, either. Something died in me when you left. The babies helped, they filled the part of my heart that longed to be a mother, but there's always been this other, empty place that nothing could fill." There was passion and anger in her look now, and in her voice. "I've hated you for that, Chance, for spoiling it for me with anyone else."

Her words pleased him, even though they weren't intended to. And he knew so well what she meant. "Me, too," he confessed. "That's exactly what it's been like for me. No one was you, Reen, so no one was right. That's why this time, we'll make the right choices. We're strong, stubborn people, but we're also older and wiser. Maybe we had to do the wrong thing before we could be sure what the right one was."

She closed her eyes again and rested her head on his shoulder. After a few moments, he felt her body shudder and then relax into exhausted sleep, and he sat immobile, willing her to rest as long as her troubled mind would allow.

Logs collapsed in the fireplace, but she didn't stir. He could smell her hair and her skin, and he breathed the sweet, familiar odors deep into his lungs. How many times since their divorce had he dreamed of this, dreamed that he was holding her as she slept. He used to awaken, and for a split second still feel the sweet weight of her head in the hollow of his shoulder, the scent of their lovemaking lingering faintly in his nostrils.

But this was no dream. This was a nightmare. The daughters he'd never had the opportunity to know were in the hands of a madman. But even nightmares could have a tiny glimmer of good in them, he reflected, if they included making love and then sitting here with his beloved in his arms as the slow, small hours of the night turned the corner to morning.

His eyes burned with weariness, and his head began to nod. After a time he pulled an afghan over them both, settled Maureen more comfortably against him, rested his head on the high back of the sofa and slid into a troubled sleep.

CHAPTER ELEVEN

KEEGAN WOKE BEFORE DAWN, his stomach rolling. He tumbled out of bed and hurried down the hall to the bathroom. He'd felt this same way when his mom died, stomach sick, head aching, mind racing from one scary black disaster to the next. And he'd felt mad then, too, although he was never quite sure what he was mad about.

He'd felt then just as he did now, that what had happened was his fault, that if he'd been smarter or nicer or different, somehow he could have prevented his mother from dying, and his cousins from getting kidnapped.

Keegan knew what it was like to be kidnapped. He and his dad's new wife, Beth, had almost been killed that summer by a crazy lady who hated Beth. Luckily his dad had arrived with the police just in time.

Why did such awful things keep happening to him? Some of his friends' parents got divorced, one of them had a sister who was mentally challenged, but nobody died or got kidnapped.

It had to be him, it had to be something he was doing that was wrong.

Clutching his belly, he huddled on the toilet in utter

misery, longing for his mom. He'd been able to talk to his mom, tell her things he couldn't tell anybody else, not even his dad.

His father had talked to him when his mom died, telling him over and over that it wasn't his fault, that there was nothing Keegan could have done to prevent the car accident.

Talking to his dad hadn't helped. For a long time Keegan had stayed angry. He hadn't wanted to come to Cooper's Corner, but he could see now that being here was the thing that had gotten him feeling better. He'd made friends, he'd started enjoying school again. He'd stopped crying for his mom, although he still missed her a lot. And he really liked Beth, the woman his dad had married. She understood about Keegan's mom. She'd taken him aside and they'd had a long talk. She'd said that nobody would ever take the place of his mom, which was true. All she wanted was to be his friend, and that had felt good.

This time, though, Keegan knew for certain that no amount of talking would make him feel better. The twins getting kidnapped was *his* fault. No way around it, he was to blame this time for sure.

A wave of nausea rolled over him again, and he moaned aloud.

He'd been told to watch them, the accusing voice in his head nagged. The kidnapping was his fault, and even if it wouldn't help, he longed to tell his dad about it. He wanted his dad here so much he could hardly stand it.

Aunt Maureen had told him why he couldn't phone

his father and tell him. It was too dangerous. But understanding why didn't stop him from wanting to do it.

He heard the puppy whining in his room, and he finally was able to get off the toilet. He splashed soap and water on his face and hands. Back in his room, he pulled on jeans and a sweatshirt and tied a piece of rope to the puppy's collar. He had to get out, he had to get away. Outside, dawn was just starting to turn the sky pink.

With the puppy in his arms, he tiptoed down the stairs. He glanced into the gathering room and saw his uncle Chance on the sofa, his arms around Aunt Maureen. They were half sitting up but they were both asleep, and their faces looked tired and lots older than they had yesterday.

For a moment he thought of waking them up, telling them how sick he was, how sorry he felt about everything, but of course he couldn't do that. It was his fault they were sitting there like that instead of being in bed.

He grabbed his jacket from the hanger by the kitchen door and put it on. Holding Satin against his chest, he went out the kitchen door and down the deck stairs.

The door to the shed still stood open, swinging wide on its hinges, another reminder of his guilt. He got the heaves in the yard, but there was nothing in his belly to bring up. His muscles hurt, though, and when it was over he ran toward the driveway leading down to the main road, holding the puppy with both arms against his chest.

Satin whined and licked at the tears running down his cheeks, and after a few minutes Keegan slowed to a walk. He wandered over to the village green, sobbing so hard he could hardly see. Luckily it was too early for anyone else to be out in the village.

He couldn't go back to Twin Oaks. No matter how well his aunt and uncle might hide it, he knew how they must feel about him letting Randi and Robin get taken like that. They might pretend not to, but he was sure they hated him. Since he couldn't call his father, and he had nowhere else to go, there was only one thing left to do.

He'd have to run away. He knew some guys in New York—maybe they'd let him stay with them. He should head for the highway, try to get a ride, but instead he ran toward the woods. He'd hide out for a while, until his stomach felt better.

Then he'd get out of Cooper's Corner forever.

TRUDI KARR PUT ON HER WORN jacket and slipped quietly out the side door of the Tubbs' house. She shivered in the early morning chill. It was just beginning to get light out, and there was hardly a sound in the town. A dog barked somewhere, and birds chirped, but there weren't any people around. Trudi liked it that way.

It would be a long time yet before the café opened for business. These early hours were the only ones in the day that belonged solely to her, and they'd become the time she looked forward to the most.

Jon would be waiting in the old orchard south of town, the way he had every morning for several weeks now. Trudi hurried along the quiet back streets, eager to see him.

She'd never trusted a man before, she'd had good reason not to. But she was beginning to trust Jon, a little, anyway. She'd never seen a man so gentle with animals. He talked to his dog in the same quiet voice he used with Trudi. She'd never heard him raise his voice, not to the dog, and not to her, either.

They'd met because of the puppies. He'd come to the café one morning when Trudi was polishing the glass on the front window, the way Lori Tubb had taught her. He was holding the cutest little dog in the crook of his arm, and he'd asked in his quiet, gentle way if Trudi knew anyone who wanted a puppy.

"Nope," Trudi said, thinking all the time that she'd love one herself. But there was no way she could take care of a puppy. If the Tubbs hadn't taken her in, she'd have had a hard time looking after herself.

She'd pretended to be polishing the window that morning, but she'd really been studying his reflection in the glass.

"First impressions are everything," Lori Tubb had told her when she explained about cleaning the window every morning. "You never get a second chance to make a first impression."

Lori knew lots of sayings like that. Trudi wondered where she got them from.

"Folks might not realize why it is," Lori told Trudi, "but if the front window is filthy, they sorta get the feeling the food might not be carefully prepared or clean. That's why we shine that window till it's gleaming."

Jon had stood there that morning without saying anything, patting the puppy, waiting until there wasn't a speck of dirt left anywhere on the glass and Trudi had to turn to face him. By that time he was smiling. She'd liked his smile straight off. His eyes smiled at the same time his mouth did. Lots of people smiled at you, but all the while their eyes said something entirely different.

"My name's Jon Durham," he'd said. "You're Trudi, right? I heard someone say you were working here now. How do you like it?"

"It's okay. It's a good job. The Tubbs are really nice to me." She hadn't returned his smile because she was suspicious of him. You never knew about men. They could pretend to be one way and then turn on you, quick as that. But in spite of herself she'd gone on looking at him. He was good to look at.

He wasn't handsome like movie stars were, and he wasn't all that tall, either, which suited her fine. Trudi didn't like men who towered over her. They scared her. The thing she noticed about him was his clear blue eyes, as blue as the sky on a windy fall morning like this one was turning out to be.

And the second thing was how clean he was. His green sweater had a couple of holes on the elbows, and his jeans were faded, but they were freshly

washed, and even his face had a scrubbed look. Lori
Tubb would approve, Trudi thought with a tiny smile.
Lori really liked clean things.

Cleanliness is next to godliness. That was another
one of Lori's pet sayings.

Lori had taught her so much, Trudi thought now,
kicking at the fallen leaves that covered the path. Nobody had ever bothered to tell Trudi things like the
importance of keeping windows clean, or that it was
wise to wash your hair every day if it was a little oily,
the way Trudi's was. And other stuff about personal
hygiene that Trudi hadn't known because her mother
died too soon to let her in on women things. Lori had
such a kind way of teaching, never saying anything
was wrong, just quietly suggesting another, better way.

Trudi thought the Tubbs were probably what it
would be like to have grandparents. She'd never had
any. Her mother had been an orphan and her father,
her real father, had taken off when she was a baby,
never to be heard from again. At least that's what her
mom had told her.

Trudi used to imagine that her father had meant to
come back, but something had happened that he
couldn't. Maybe there'd been an accident that had
caused him to lose his memory, or maybe he'd gotten
killed and nobody knew who he was, so they couldn't
tell her mother she was a widow.

She and her mom had managed okay, up until the
time Trudi was eight. That was when her mom had
gotten a divorce and married again.

Trudi shuddered, remembering. She'd hated and

feared her stepfather from the moment she first laid eyes on him, but her mom had been blind and deaf to anything Trudi said. She'd cuffed her across the mouth hard when Trudi said he was too old and that his boys were mean to her. The only good thing had been when her mom got pregnant and Trudi had a beautiful baby brother, someone she could really love. But then her mom had up and died and left her alone with her stepfather and his awful older sons.

Trudi shoved that sickening memory to the back of her mind now, noticing instead the brilliance of the leaves and the clear freshness of the morning air. It was going to be a sunny day. The sky was turning pink in the east, and birds were singing their crazy lungs out. Funny how here in the country she noticed things like that, while in the city she'd never paid any attention to the weather or the sky, except to curse when it was raining or snowing. She couldn't remember any birds, either, although she knew there had to have been some.

She came to the clearing, and Jon was waiting just like she knew he would be, standing by the big old sugar maple at the edge of the orchard where his trailer was parked. Sheba came bounding through the dried grass, two puppies yelping and tumbling along at her heels.

"Hey, Speedy. Hi, Bonzo." Trudi greeted the babies, crouching down and patting them before she hugged their mother, Sheba. The dog's tongue was rough against her cheek and she giggled. She couldn't remember ever laughing as much as she had with Jon at these dogs.

"I'm clean, Sheba, you don't need to wash me. You've got enough to do with these rascals." She ran her hands through the puppy's silky fur. They rolled over, legs waving in the air, so she could rub their fat, bare bellies.

She saw Jon walking over, and when he was beside her, she got to her feet and smiled at him, feeling shy the way she always did at first.

"I've got coffee on. Want some?" He reached out a hand and she put her own in his, aware of the big, rough palm and the callused fingers gently encircling hers.

"It's going to be a fine day," he remarked as they strolled toward the trailer. The puppies bit at their ankles and tried to trip them, and Jon finally told Sheba to take them away.

Trudi was still amazed at the way Jon could make Sheba understand exactly what he wanted her to do, just by using a few quiet commands. He'd explained that she was a dog who wanted to please, and that she'd been easier than most to train. There were some dogs, though, that resisted, and they took more effort and time to train than Sheba had. He figured Speedy was going to be one of those dogs, independent and headstrong. Stubborn.

Trudi thought the way Jon trained dogs was the way people oughta be with kids, talking to them gentle and not hitting them when they made mistakes.

"Are you working today, Jon?" His hair shone gold

in the sun that had just risen over the eastern hills. Sometimes she wished this was all there was to life, walking along in the early morning with him, hand in hand, dogs frolicking nearby, the two of them chatting about their jobs and the coming day.

"Yup. I'm finishing the gables on the Goodmans' house this morning. Seth's got an estimate to do on a garage conversion over in New Ashford. He'll need to have plumbing done so he's taking Bonnie with him."

Trudi had been fascinated by the fact that the local plumber was a woman. She'd never thought about women having jobs as carpenters or plumbers. It had started her thinking a lot about the ways people earned their living, and she'd thought that she wouldn't mind being a carpenter, working outside. Jon said it got cold sometimes, or wet when it rained, and some of it was hard physical work, but it would be better than dealing with people all day, the way she did in the café. Not that the people in the village were anything but nice to her. It was just that she wasn't used to people talking to her, joking and teasing and expecting a response all the time. It made her uneasy.

Jon opened the door of the trailer and waited while she stepped inside. That was another thing she liked about him, that he was so polite. On the rag rug by the door, she slid her feet out of her runners. Jon kept the trailer as clean as he kept himself.

"You hear about the kids at Twin Oaks getting kidnapped yesterday?" He was at the counter pouring hot coffee from his coffeemaker into thick brown mugs.

"Yeah. I heard." She wished she didn't know. She

sat down on the little sofa, and her stomach tightened. Since she woke up she'd been trying not to think about those poor sweet little girls or the danger they were in.

"The Tubbs told me, but they warned me not to say anything to anybody." Suddenly the world wasn't as shiny as it had been moments before. "They said that somebody told Ms. Cooper on the phone not to say anything to anybody because—" She gulped and couldn't finish. "How did you find out, Jon?"

"I was in the general store when the vet came in, right after it happened. He'd already been to Tubb's. He was asking if anyone saw anything strange, and he said the twins had disappeared." Jon handed her a mug, already fixed with cream and two sugars the way she liked it. "Then I heard later that they'd been kidnapped. Sounds as if whoever took them means business."

She nodded, taking a swallow of coffee too soon, gasping as it burned its hot way to her empty belly.

"Poor little kids." Tears gathered behind her eyes. Why did it always have to be little kids that suffered? Anger mingled with the coffee in her gut and all of a sudden she felt nauseous.

"You got any idea what it's all about? I mean, why would somebody snatch a couple of kids in a little place like this? All I can figure is somebody real nasty's got it in for Ms. Cooper."

"I guess." Trudi nodded, feeling more miserable by the second.

"What are folks saying in the café?"

Trudi felt uneasy all of a sudden. Her old suspicions came tumbling back into her head. Jon was asking so many questions. Maybe he had reasons she knew nothing about. What did she really know about him, anyway? What if...?

"Why are you so interested?" The question came out sounding belligerent, and she saw the surprise on his face.

"Aren't you?" He said it in his usual gentle tone, but now she was spooked. "It's a big thing, having kids kidnapped in a place like this."

"I—I'm scared for those kids," she stammered. "I'm scared for Ms. Cooper. She's a really nice lady. She was good to me after—"

He knew her story. She hadn't talked about it with him, but in Cooper's Corner, everyone seemed to know everybody else's story.

"You think that guy who gave you the drugs is the same guy behind this? What was his name? Nesbitt?"

"Nevil. Owen Nevil. What are you, an undercover cop or something?"

He laughed and shook his head, refusing to take offense. "You're way off base, Trudi. I'm no cop, far from it. Truth be told, cops make me real nervous."

"You been in trouble with the law?" He didn't seem the type.

"Oh, yeah." He nodded and his blond hair fell down over his forehead. She longed to push it back, and blushed as if he could tell what she was thinking.

"I was pretty heavy into drugs when I was younger," he confessed. "I got charged in juvenile court, put on probation. And there was other stuff, worse stuff, but I was lucky, because I didn't get caught.''

''What kind of other stuff?'' She felt apprehensive, no longer at ease with him. Why did everyone have to have a dark side? She'd wanted to believe that Jon was different, that he was innocent, that the darkness hadn't touched him. She felt betrayed.

''Oh, stuff dumb young guys get into—break and enter, petty theft. I moved up here to get away from the gang I was with in the city. They were older, a real rough bunch, and they figured I owed them when I tried to break away. They'd arranged a lawyer for me and stuff for the drug charge, and they said I had to pay them back. That would have meant a whole new barrel of trouble, so I split.''

''Do they know where you are?''

He didn't meet her eyes. His voice sounded troubled. ''I thought they didn't. But last week, one of them tracked me down.'' He finished his coffee, got up and put the mug in the tiny sink. He didn't turn to look at her.

''I may have to leave Cooper's Corner, Trudi, and I might have to go fast. I'm not sure I'll be able to let you know ahead of time. These guys are tough, and I'd rather not stick around and let them surprise me.''

''You don't owe me anything.'' A peculiar emptiness had taken the place of the nausea, and she used the tough voice she'd perfected when she didn't want people to know she was hurting.

''It's not a case of owing. We get along, you and I.

I really like being around you.'' He paused and then added in an offhand tone, ''I guess you wouldn't want to come with me?''

''With? With—with you?'' She swallowed hard. ''When you go, you mean?''

''Yeah.'' He watched her, and her face must have shown him what she was thinking, because he shrugged.

''Hey, you don't have to say anything. Maybe it's not such a hot idea. I mean, I couldn't take this trailer, anyway. I just rent it from old man Thorsson. And I've got to find a home for those other two puppies before I go anywhere. You can't be on the road with a dog and two pups. Being on the road wouldn't be much of a life for a girl.''

She longed to be on the road with him. Misery almost choked her. ''Yeah. Right. Well. I'd like to, but I couldn't. Come with you, I mean. I've got—''

''Obligations. Absolutely. I know that. You've got a good job and a place to stay and people you like.'' For a moment he looked as miserable as she felt. ''Like I said, it was a bummer of an idea. A person can't just walk away on all that.''

She would in a minute, except for— But she couldn't explain, it was way too complicated. Getting up, she set her cup carefully in the sink, beside his.

''I've gotta go. I have to shower and change before I go to work.'' She shoved her feet in her shoes and bent to tie them. Then she opened the door and stepped out. ''Bye, Jon.''

He put his own shoes on and followed her outside,

stood beside her on the damp grass. The sun was up, steam was rising from the meadow. It was going to be a clear, sunny day.

"See you tomorrow morning, Trudi?"

It was the first time he'd asked. The uncertainty in his voice tore at her heart.

She tried to smile at him. "I hope so. If you're still here." It was the only answer she could give. Nothing was certain in her world or in his.

"I won't be going that soon." He stepped closer to her and her heart seemed to stop. He used a finger to tilt her head up, and then he lowered his head and kissed her.

His lips were soft. She knew hers were chapped. She was glad she'd brushed her teeth before she came. And after an instant, none of that mattered, because warmth uncurled in her belly and a feeling of safety and excitement blossomed inside of her.

When the kiss ended, he held her for a long time, and she didn't want to move or say anything because it felt so good, better than any feelings she could remember having.

At last he dropped his arms and took a step back, but then he raised his hand and traced the line of her jaw with a finger.

"You're so pretty, Trudi." He said it in a plain, matter-of-fact voice that meant he really thought so. It sent a thrill shooting right through her.

No one had ever told her that before. In her entire life, no one had ever said she was pretty. Mrs. Tubb had said she looked nice in the two dresses she'd

bought for Trudi to wear in the café, and once her
mother had said she was lucky to have such long eyelashes. But that was a long way from being pretty.

Like a dork, she couldn't even answer him. She just
blushed and nodded and then turned on her heel and
ran. At the edge of the orchard, she stopped and
turned. He was standing there as if he was waiting,
and when he saw her stop, he waved. She waved back
and then she ran again.

She couldn't go straight back to the Tubbs' house.
They'd talk to her, ask her questions in their kind,
nosy way about where she'd been and who she'd seen
and what kind of day did she think it was going to be.
They were the talkingest people she'd ever met, and
mostly she didn't mind.

But right now she needed to be quiet and alone for
a while. She needed to savor what had just happened,
put it into a special place in her head so she could
take it out again and again.

She ran hard, and when she came to the woods she
slowed and walked instead, her heart still hammering,
more from the kiss than from running.

It was cold and wet among the trees. She drew in
deep lungfuls of air and let them out again. Sometimes
she felt as if she'd never really breathed deep in her
chest until she came to Cooper's Corner. The air in
the city wasn't the kind that made you want to draw
it into your lungs.

She walked slowly, and instead of thinking, she just
let herself feel for once. There was sadness and disappointment because Jon was leaving. Whatever you

liked always got taken away, in her experience. There was pleasure at his kiss, frustration and anger because she couldn't go with him. She never got to do anything she wanted to do. Sometimes it seemed as if her whole life had been decided by other people.

She hardly noticed the fear. She'd felt it for so long, trying her best to ignore it or bury it beneath other things. But it was always there, just beneath the surface, ready to jump out like one of the horrible monsters in late-night movies.

Behind her, a branch cracked and a small animal cried out in pain.

Someone was running straight toward her, crashing through the underbrush, making noises like snorts. Her breath caught in her throat and her heart raced.

She wanted to run but her legs felt like jelly, and she was too scared to even scream. She got behind a tree. It was too small to hide her, but there was nothing else she could do.

CHAPTER TWELVE

THE PUPPY WAS YELPING, and Keegan realized he was holding her too tight. He loosened his hold and slowed to a walk, swiping with his hand at the tears and snot that made his face wet and itchy.

Satin struggled to get down, and he bent and placed her on the leaves. She crouched and peed, and then dived at his shoe and started growling and chewing on his laces.

"Goofy girl." Having her with him was good. He didn't feel quite so alone.

"Keegan?"

He jumped and cried out in fright. He hadn't thought anyone else was around.

Trudi Karr stepped out from behind a tree.

"Sorry, Keegan. You scared me, too, when I heard you running this way a minute ago."

He sniffed hard, hoping she wouldn't know that he'd been crying.

"Out for a walk with the puppy?"

He nodded. He knew by the way she was looking at him that she'd noticed the tears. He didn't have a tissue, so he sniffed again a couple of times.

Trudi dug a crumbled paper napkin out of her jacket pocket and held it out to him. He blew his nose hard.

"I guess you're feeling bad about your cousins getting taken like that yesterday."

"Yeah." His aunt hadn't said anything about not talking with people who already knew. "It was all my fault. I shouldn't have let it happen." To his horror, he started crying again, gulping and choking. He couldn't stop.

Trudi just stood and waited until he could control himself, and then she said in that quiet, flat way she had, "What the heck makes you think that it was your fault?"

"I was—I was supposed to be watching them. I went to the bathroom, just for a couple minutes, and when I got back they—they were gone." The sounds that came out of him were making Satin anxious. She whimpered and tried to climb up his leg.

Trudi knelt down and played with the puppy, finding the spot behind her ears that sent her into some kind of wriggling trance.

"It wasn't your fault," she said in a definite voice, looking up at Keegan and scowling at him as if she was angry. "Bad things just happen. You can't go around blaming yourself for stuff all the time."

"But they're…they're probably gonna d-die." He could hardly bear to say it out loud.

"That's garbage." She sounded angry. "People just say that to scare you. They'd never do it."

Keegan shook his head. "You're wrong. I know they're gonna die. I heard my uncle Chance talking to Dr. Dorn. They were saying that when there's nobody asking for ransom money, it doesn't look good, and I know what they meant. What does this guy want if he doesn't want money? The girls are gonna die, and it'll be my fault, for my whole life.''

Trudi shot to her feet, and for a moment Keegan thought she was going to slap him. ''Don't you say that, don't you *ever* say that,'' she shrieked at him. ''Nobody's gonna die. You get that out of your stupid head this minute.''

Shocked and feeling betrayed by her, he stumbled back a step or two.

''What do you know about it?'' he hollered back at her. ''They're not *your* cousins. You don't know how it feels.'' He snatched up Satin and took off at a full run, winding through the trees.

''Keegan. Keegan, come back, I'm sorry.'' He could hear her hollering after him, and he knew that she chased him for a while, but she was no match for him when it came to running.

Soon her voice faded, and when he was certain he'd lost her, he slowed to a walk and then collapsed on the bank of a stream, winded. He was too exhausted mentally and physically to do anything more than scoop up water in his hands and drink until at last his thirst was eased.

Satin, too, lapped water, almost tumbling into the creek on her first attempts. When she, too, had had enough, she burped loudly and then curled up beside him and fell asleep. The sun was well up by now, and the frost of the morning was gone. The earth was still damp, but the sunshine on his face and body was warm and comforting. Keegan took off his jacket and put it under his head. He pressed his face against Satin's side, taking comfort from her sweet puppy smell and the rapid beating of her heart, and before long, he, too, slept.

MAUREEN WOKE TO THE SOUND of a telephone ringing.

She leaped up, heart racing, coming out of confusing dreams to a reality too horrible to contemplate.

She lunged for the telephone.

"Yes? Hello?"

But there was only a dial tone, and the phone was still ringing.

"Easy, Reen. It's my cell." Chance dug a small folding unit from his pants pocket and flipped it open.

"Hello, Wally," Maureen heard him say.

Her heart was pounding at a pace that frightened her. She pressed a hand to her chest and collapsed back on the sofa, where she'd been curled in Chance's arms. Disappointment made her feel ill.

"Look, Wally, I've got a situation here, and I can't—" Chance stopped and listened. Maureen could hear a male voice, raised and indignant, coming from the cell.

She could also hear muted sounds from the kitchen, smell coffee brewing and bacon frying. But instead of hunger, she felt revulsion.

Even in her sleep, she hadn't forgotten for an instant, and she had an irrational urge to just open her mouth and start to scream, to stop trying to be strong and just allow the hysteria she'd battened down to surface and take over.

It was Chance's presence that stopped her, as it had the night before. He glanced at her, winked and slid a muscular arm around her shoulders, squeezing her tight in a hug, pressing a kiss on her forehead even as he said into the receiver in a no-nonsense tone, "Wally, your only responsibility is to be a diplomat and help pull that department out of the slump it's in. I don't give a damn what your conflicts are with Lindsey Armstrong—"

He stopped and listened again.

"She's *pregnant?*"

Maureen tried to get up, because obviously he was having a very personal conversation. Chance shook his head and held on to her.

"Is there a possibility that it's your child, Wally?" He listened again.

"Well, if she wanted you to father a child for her, she must have *some* feelings for you, whether or not she told you what she was doing. I know you feel used, but if you care about her, then talk to her, Wally."

For what seemed a long time he listened to the person on the other end. Then, in an impatient voice, he ordered, "Shut up and listen to me, and listen good. Forget pride, forget temper, get over feeling tricked. Go to her and tell her the absolute truth about how you really feel. If you have feelings for the woman, tell her you do." Chance's voice rang with conviction. He took a handful of Maureen's hair and let it slide through his fingers.

"Believe me, I know what I'm talking about here.

And if you have a choice between being right and being kind, be kind, Wally. Give her the benefit of the doubt. If the baby's yours, you'll want to be around for the long haul, believe me. So do whatever it takes to make peace."

After another few minutes he hung up and muttered, "God, I wish someone had given me that advice a few years back."

Maureen was thinking how much he'd changed. Chance had always needed to be right, needed to win every argument. Maureen knew she had the same compulsion. In that way, too, they were alike, and it had destroyed them.

If they tried again, could she take the advice he'd just given his friend? Could she put aside her temper, her ego, in order to make their relationship work?

She wasn't sure. She wasn't sure of anything right now, except that she somehow had to get her babies home safely. After that, she'd be able to think about the rest of her life.

As she breathed in the scent of last night's love-making, she wondered if she hadn't made a terrible mistake. He'd been back in her life for less than a day, and how could she be certain of anything just now? She felt terrible. Her neck was stiff, her entire body hurt as if she'd been in an accident or a fight. She moved to ease the pain in her muscles.

Chance ended the conversation and folded up his phone, sticking it back in his pocket. When he looked at her, his blue eyes were bleary and bloodshot, and she could see the toll this was taking on him as well.

"You slept," he said to her, rubbing a hand through her hair and bringing her face up against his. She could feel his morning whiskers against her cheek, and she closed her eyes for a moment longer, savoring the closeness. She'd needed him so badly, and he'd given her a few moments of release. She'd take that and try not to think beyond it.

"I need a shower," she sighed. "But I'm scared to have one in case the phone rings."

"I'll listen for the phone while you're in the shower," he offered. "Then I'll have a shower and shave." He rubbed a hand over his jaw. "My overnight bag's still in the front hallway. Maybe you could show me which room to use?"

There were plenty of empty guest rooms at Twin Oaks, but she led him to her own bedroom.

She saw the acknowledgement and gratitude in the look he gave her as he glanced around, realized it was her bedroom, and set his bag on the old trunk at the foot of her bed. The bed was queen-size, covered in a colorful patchwork quilt. There was a rocking chair by the window. She'd made the ruffled green chintz curtains at the window.

Suddenly she was shy.

"There's a phone on the nightstand there, but I can't hear it in the shower."

"I'll be right here listening for it. You go ahead, and take your time."

She gestured at a half-open door in the corner.

"That's the twins' bedroom." She had to swallow hard as she showed him their daughters' room.

Two child-size cots, covered in fluffy embroidered white duvets, were pushed close together, littered with soft teddies and stuffed animals. A toy box under a window overflowed with dolls and trucks and hand-made wooden toys. A soft yellow rug covered the floor, and out of the half-open drawer of a large antique dresser spilled miniature blue jeans and tiny T-shirts. A little pink sock lay discarded on the rocking chair, and a half-completed wooden puzzle was scattered across the wide window seat.

The empty room spoke more eloquently of the twins' absence than anything else had, and her heart contracted.

Chance stood and gazed in, then turned to her and took her in his arms. "They'll be sleeping here tonight, Reen."

She knew his words were more like a prayer than a promise.

Standing under the hot shower spray a short time later, she took comfort from the warmth and the sense of cleanliness it provided. When she went back into the bedroom, wrapped in her old white terry robe, she gave Chance a questioning look and gestured at the phone. "It didn't ring?"

"Not yet."

She bit her lip and shook her head, struggling with an overwhelming sense of despair.

"What if—what if he never calls again? What if the girls just disappear? I had a case once where exactly that happened. This little boy just disappeared, and we never found any trace of him." She could hear hysteria in her own voice as she recalled the mother's anguish, the father's rage. She understood it, how well she understood it now.

"Soon, Reen. He'll call soon. He's playing games with us."

He was right, she knew it. She blew out a frustrated breath, and he came over and gave her a hug.

Maureen looked up at him, at his tired, bloodshot eyes, his strong, chiseled features. She'd judged every man she'd met since their divorce by him, and she'd found every one wanting.

"I don't know how I'd have gotten through this without you, Chance."

"It means everything to me to be here." He stroked a finger down her cheek, pushed her wet hair behind her ear.

"Today's going to be bad."

He didn't deny it. "Yeah, it is. You'll let me know if there's anything at all I can do to make it easier for you, okay?"

She nodded. "Right now, I need a cup of coffee. I feel like I could use the caffeine."

"I'll go down and get us each one." He left, and Maureen hurried into fresh underwear, jeans and a long-sleeved checked flannel shirt. By the time he got back with two mugs of coffee, she was once again pacing back and forth, praying for the phone to ring.

He smiled at her and handed her a mug. "Harry and Lydia are down there making a breakfast that only a team of lumberjacks could do justice to."

Her coffee was fixed just the way she liked it, cream

and no sugar. He'd remembered after all this time, and that gave her a tiny pang of pleasure.

"They're really fixated on this food thing, but I just can't eat," she said. Although it tasted good, even the coffee seemed to burn a hole in the lining of her stomach. "I'm not hungry." Food was about the last thing on her mind just now.

He came over and took her by the shoulders. "You do need to eat, Reen. We both do. We're going to need every ounce of strength to get through this, and being weak from hunger won't help."

She gave a reluctant nod. She knew he was right, and when he'd showered and her coffee was gone, she followed him down to the kitchen, glancing at the big wooden clock on the wall above the refrigerator. It was ten to eight. The twins had been gone twenty-two hours. A feeling of hopelessness and utter terror came over her.

Would she ever see her babies again? What was happening to them at this moment? She thought of the endless unspeakable acts committed against children, and shuddered.

"Don't go there, Reen." Chance was watching her, and he spoke softly. "We'll hear soon, we'll get them back. Just go on believing that."

He'd always been able to guess what she was thinking. It had been one of the amazing things about their relationship, that each often knew what the other was thinking or about to say.

At this moment, he didn't know any more than she did, but his assurance comforted and calmed her.

Downstairs, she was able to greet Harry and Lydia, compliment them on how organized the kitchen looked. It smelled good, of fresh biscuits, strong coffee, bacon, eggs, pancakes, but when Lydia set a platter in front of her, Maureen's stomach rebelled. All she was able to choke down was a small bowl of fruit salad and half a slice of toast, and the whole time she forced herself to chew and swallow, she thought of Randi and Robin.

Had they been given anything to eat this morning? Had anyone washed them, brushed their hair, told them to clean their teeth? In some weird fashion, Maureen felt that by being clean, by taking pleasure last night in making love, even by eating, she was somehow betraying her daughters. She knew it was irrational, crazy even, but she felt it, anyway. The lump of toast stuck in her throat and she pushed the plate away. Eating another bite was impossible.

"Is there anything at all you fancy?" Lydia Joyce's face creased with worry as she eyed the minute amount of food Maureen had eaten. "Anything at all you think you could stomach, Harry and I can make for you. I mean, the neighbors have brought soup and casseroles, things like that, but if you'd like an omelet, French toast, maybe some broth…?"

"No. Nothing, thank you all the same." Maureen gathered the shreds of her composure and forced something that should have been a smile. She couldn't stand the thought of food just now. "Has Keegan eaten already? Has he fed the puppy yet?" Even though Chance had said it was all right, Keegan had

double-checked with Maureen as to whether he could
take Satin to his bedroom last night.

She'd told him it was a good idea. She knew her
nephew felt responsible for the loss of the twins, and
she wanted to talk to him this morning, assure him
that he was totally blameless.

Both Lydia and Harry shook their heads. "We
haven't seen either the boy or the puppy yet today.
Maybe they're having a good long sleep."

But Maureen had never known Keegan to sleep in
and miss breakfast, and it seemed unlikely he'd choose
this particular morning to do it. Besides, the puppy
would have been whining for food long before now.
A new anxiety niggled at her.

"I'll just go up and check on them." Maureen
headed for Clint and Keegan's suite. She opened Keegan's bedroom door as quietly as she could, in case
he was still sleeping, but the room was empty. Clint
had left her in charge of his son. She'd been so distracted since yesterday morning that she'd hardly said
more than a few words to her nephew. When bad
things happened, was there some rule about more following?

She shoved the thought away and went slowly back
down the hall, trying to think where Keegan might
have gone. It seemed unlikely, the way things were,
that he'd go anywhere without telling someone. She
felt a sharp stab of irritation at him. He knew how
horribly worried she was, and had no business worrying her further.

She stopped abruptly and slumped against the wall,

wrapping her arms around her. Was she, on some level, blaming Keegan for leaving the twins unattended? With her brain, she knew how unfair and wrong that was, but her heart was a different matter. It was hard to do, but she admitted that she *did* feel resentment toward him.

He was a sensitive boy, he'd have picked up on it. A surge of new terror went through her. He already blamed himself and didn't need her piling guilt on him. Where had he gone? Why hadn't he come back? How long had he been away?

"Oh, God, Clint," she whispered under her breath. "Not your son, too. We can't lose Keegan as well."

She straightened and raced back to the kitchen, startling the Joyces.

Chance saw the panicked expression on her face and hurried over to her. "What is it?"

"He's not in his room, Chance. Keegan's gone. The puppy's gone, too," she blurted.

"Maybe he's just taken Satin for a walk," Chance said.

"No. I don't think so. I'm worried about him. I'm afraid he thinks I blame him for what happened with the girls."

Chance didn't deny it. "Would you feel better if I went out and had a look around for him?"

"Oh, would you, please? I'm worried sick about him, and I need to stay by the phone."

Grabbing his jacket, Chance hurried out.

CHAPTER THIRTEEN

THERE WEREN'T MANY PEOPLE out this early on a Saturday morning in Cooper's Corner. The few Chance met were quick to inquire whether he and Maureen had heard anything yet. They followed the query with the assurance that they hadn't told a living, breathing soul, and no, they hadn't seen Keegan this morning.

Trevor came by on his bike, and Chance stopped him.

"Did Keegan maybe go with you this morning on your paper route, Trevor?"

"No, sir. I haven't seen him since yesterday." The boy looked around and then in a stage whisper asked about the twins. Chance told him there was no news.

"Right now I really need to find Keegan," he told Trevor. "Could you see if you can spot him for me? Tell him Maureen needs him at Twin Oaks."

Chance had thought he'd find Keegan wandering around with the puppy, but now he was beginning to worry about the boy. Where the hell could he be?

"Sure thing, Mr. Maguire. I'll find him." Trevor went flying off on his bike, and Chance spotted a young woman in a blue-checked shirtwaist dress cleaning the front window of Tubb's Café with a handful of paper towels and a spray bottle. He remembered what Maureen had told him and guessed that this was Trudi Karr.

He walked up to her and gave her a friendly smile, assessing the nervous glance she shot him and the way she edged away, even though he wasn't standing anywhere near her.

"My name is Chance Maguire, and I'm looking for my nephew, Keegan Cooper. I wonder if you've seen him this morning?"

The bottle of cleanser dropped from her hand. Fortunately it was plastic and didn't break on the sidewalk, but he caught the frightened expression on her face when he picked it up and handed it to her.

"I—I saw him before, but I just thought he was going home," she said in a voice that trembled.

"Where exactly did you see him?"

She lifted a hand and pointed. Chance noticed that her fingernails were bitten to the quick.

"Up the hill a ways, over in the woods."

"Was he walking the dog? How far away was he?"

"He—well, he was quite a long ways. He had Sheba's puppy with him and the last I saw of him he was running."

"Running?" Chance frowned. "Running where? Why was he running, do you think?"

She wouldn't look at him. Her face had gone red, and she stared past him, at the café door. For a few minutes she didn't say anything, and then she blurted, "We had sort of an argument. I said something I shouldn't have and he took off. I tried to catch him but I couldn't—he's a real fast runner. And I thought he'd head back toward the village, anyhow," she said in a defensive tone. "I just naturally thought he'd go home." She gave Chance another nervous glance. "That's why I didn't come to Twin Oaks and tell anybody. I thought about it, but I just figured he'd go home."

"What time was this?"

"Early. Prob'ly seven. The sun was just coming up."

"What's your name?" He thought he knew, but he wanted to be certain.

"Trudi. Trudi Karr."

She looked both miserable and scared. She still wouldn't meet his eyes. Was she the one who had acted as a spy for whoever had taken his daughters?

A surge of anger made Chance want to take her by the shoulders and shake her—shake until the truth came tumbling out of her. Instead, he opened the café door and gestured her inside.

"Maybe Mrs. Tubb will give you half an hour off, and you can come and show me where you last saw Keegan, Trudi. I'm getting really worried about him— he's been gone quite a while. Let's ask her."

Lori Tubb unfortunately resembled her surname. Short, round, with a cap of hair she kept carefully dyed a shoe-polish black, she greeted Chance, took him by the arm and hauled him into the kitchen so the other patrons wouldn't hear her inquire about Maureen and the girls.

When Chance explained that there'd been no word,

and that Keegan had run off before breakfast without telling anyone where he was going, she immediately urged Trudi to go and help find him.

"Poor child, it's all been too much for him," she concluded with a sigh. "You go off and bring him back here, tell him I'll make him the cheeseburger special with onion fries he's so fond of. Food helps when you're that age."

The entire population of Cooper's Corner seemed to believe in the healing powers of food, Chance thought. There was something innocent, homey and heartening about it.

Trudi put on a green jacket hanging by the back door of the café and led the way along the village street and then up into one of the groves of sugar maples that surrounded Cooper's Corner. They walked until they came to where an old trailer sat far off in one corner of an orchard. A dog barked ferociously.

"That's Sheba. She'll be locked in the pen with the pups. Jon puts her in there while he's at work."

"Jon?"

"Jon Durham."

They were walking side by side, and Chance saw the flush that stained the girl's fair skin. He recalled the name from the list of people Maureen had shown him. Jon was the one who'd been charged as a juvenile for possession, he remembered.

"Jon lives there, but his pickup is gone, so he'll be at work. He's a carpenter."

Trudi headed across the orchard to a place where the trees gave way to a more thickly wooded area, and walked quickly along a well-worn, narrow path leading up a hill. Chance kept right behind her, growing more alarmed the farther they got from the village. What was Keegan doing, so far from home?

"Did Keegan seem upset when you talked to him, Trudi?"

She hesitated and then nodded. "Yeah, some."

"Did he say what he was upset about?"

She turned and gave him a look, as if he should be able to guess. "The twins," she said.

It was obvious she wasn't eager to get into a discussion with him. Chance didn't want to frighten her, but he was determined to find a way to break through her reticence.

"It was right here I last saw him." Trudi stopped in a small grove. "He went running along that path, going that way, and I chased him for a while, but he was real quick. He got away on me."

Chance shouted, *"Keegan? Keegan, where are you?"*

They both listened, but there was only an echo and no answer.

He shouted again and again, with no response, and at last Trudi turned as if to go back along the path the way they'd come.

Frustrated, and growing more concerned about his nephew by the moment, Chance reached a hand out and grabbed her arm. She flinched, and even through the jacket, her arm felt fragile, the bones as frail as a bird's.

"Trudi, stay here. I need to know exactly what you

and Keegan said to each other. Why did he run off that way?"

She twisted away from his grasp and he let her go, feeling a stab of regret and pity at the blatant fear that flickered in her eyes and on her face.

It took a moment before she answered. "I guess he figures what happened yesterday is all his fault."

Chance sighed and nodded. "I thought so. I tried to tell him that's not so."

"Yeah, me, too." She shivered and scuffed a toe in the dried leaves, her head bent. "I told him things just happen, things that we can't do anything about. But he's real scared the twins won't— He's scared—" She raised her head and Chance saw utter, bleak terror in her gaze.

"What, Trudi? What's he so scared of?" Whatever it was, she was afraid of the same thing.

"That—that the twins are gonna—" her voice faltered "—gonna *die*. That the guy who took them is gonna kill them. That he won't ever bring them back, like—like—"

Her voice trembled and she stopped abruptly, her square face ashen.

She knew something, he was positive of it. Chance struggled with a frantic primal urge to use violence to extract it. Instead, he kept his voice companionable and soft, using every shred of self-control he possessed to keep from scaring her into silence.

"Like what, Trudi? Like Nevil told you he would?"

She gave her head a vehement shake.

"I don't know anything," she jabbered.

But she did, Chance was certain of it. "Where is he, Trudi? You know where he is, don't you?"

She shook her head again even harder. "I don't know anything, just what Lori told me. She said not to say anything to anybody. And I didn't. Honest, I didn't."

"I believe you." He wasn't sure he did, but he desperately wanted her cooperation. Chance drew a deep breath and asked the question that haunted him, that he suspected she already knew the answer to.

"What do you think the kidnapper wants, Trudi? What do you think he's after? Why do you think he took the twins? He hasn't asked for money, so it has to be something else he's after. Do you know what it might be?"

"How would I know?" Her voice was sullen, and she still wouldn't look at him. "I've gotta go back now, Lori's on her own. Burt went out to help search buildings this morning, in case the twins—"

"I know, I heard what the villagers are doing." With difficulty Chance held on to the frayed edges of his temper. "I think you know more than you're willing to admit, Trudi. But right now I don't have time to convince you to tell the truth. I have to find Keegan and get back to Maureen, and I don't know these woods at all." The by-now-familiar feeling of frustration and impotence came over him. He was in a situation that he wasn't in control of, and it maddened him.

"It sounds as if Keegan wasn't in very good shape when you saw him, Trudi," he said. "There's no telling what he might do. Is there anybody else who could help me look?''

Her shoulders slumped. ''Jon would help, but he's at work. He's got Sheba, though. He told me she's a good tracker. I'll go get Sheba. Maybe she can find the trail.''

Chance watched her jog off, doubtful that she'd come back. This was probably just an excuse to get away from him. He raised his voice and called Keegan, but again there was no response.

In business, Chance was a take-charge man with little tolerance for indecision. He was bold and forthright in his management of companies and employees, and he always kept at least two alternatives in mind during any crisis situation.

And yet now, with the fate of his daughters hanging in the balance, his beloved ex-wife in grave danger and his nephew missing, he had no plan whatsoever, much less an alternative.

CHAPTER FOURTEEN

EDWARD GATON HAD DEVELOPED a plan for the times when he reached a block in his writing. He'd found that walking helped.

It had happened this morning. The words that had been dancing along since before dawn, flying from brain to fingertips to the small computer screen of his laptop, suddenly faltered, slowed, and then dried up.

The cottage he was renting was heated by wood, and as usual he'd forgotten to put another log in the compact little heater. It had gotten cold and he hadn't even noticed. He'd also forgotten to bring any wood in from the huge stack his landlord had given him.

Edward was a city man, and although as a child he'd been accustomed to wood-burning stoves and the necessity for carrying wood and water into the house, he'd long since forgotten the routine. He now viewed it as a huge pain in the derriere, but here in the isolated cabin he'd found a place to live that was not only cheap, but far enough away from people and their endless questions. And at least he had electricity to power his laptop.

Instead of lighting the fire again, he threw on his wool jacket and set off along the meandering path that led up the hillside, along the creek, and then down into Cooper's Corner. It was a route he took several times a week on his regular trips to the library.

Tubb's Café wouldn't be open for another hour, but it would take him that long at least to get there. He'd splurge and have breakfast at Tubb's, he decided, instead of just his usual coffee, because he wanted to hear the latest about the kidnapping. He'd been in the restaurant yesterday when the vet came flying in and announced that the Cooper twins had been taken.

The Coopers.

Edward sneered to himself as he strode among the trees. They were like royalty in this town that had been named after them, and it was no wonder someone would take their children and demand ransom. They were so arrogant, they'd even planted trees to commemorate the births of their children—oaks on either side of the drive leading up to the oldest surviving Cooper farmhouse, aptly named Twin Oaks. As far as he could tell, half the village had Cooper genes. They were everywhere, the Cooper clan.

And they had easy lives, these people. They knew nothing of true hardship. The world wars hadn't affected them greatly, apart from the servicemen who'd died in battle and whose names were inscribed on the memorial in town. Edward felt such anger when he read those names, such a sense of outrage that these men were viewed as heroes. They had no concept of the misery some of those men had caused in small villages and towns all over Europe.

Edward's book would reveal it all, expose certain

of those servicemen for the rogues they really were. He'd meticulously researched and located others like himself, interviewed them, taken copious notes, but when it came to writing the book, he'd found he needed to tell his own story first.

He'd had to come to Cooper's Corner and see for himself where his grandfather had lived. He'd wanted to meet the relatives who'd turned their backs on his grandmother and his mother in their time of need. It had infuriated him to discover the lush farmland and the huge houses, the relative luxury they'd enjoyed while his own family had existed in abject poverty.

His research had uncovered a great deal about the Cooper clan. There was Warren Cooper, the old man who'd died a couple of years ago, and his brother, Charles, who'd gone off to war. It was in France that Charles had met Edward's grandmother, Cecile.

Edward had been walking faster and faster, arms pumping as resentment churned in him. He burst out of the trees by the stream and stopped short.

"Mon Dieu." A lanky boy was asleep on the grass. A black-and-white puppy who'd been lying beside him jumped up and came running over to Edward, yapping and biting at his laces.

It took a moment for Edward to recognize Keegan Cooper, the same moment it took Keegan to wake up and stagger to his feet.

"What are you doing here, boy?" Edward was startled. His tone was both gruff and accusatory.

"Nothing." Keegan took several steps back and

whistled to the puppy, but the little animal went right on mouthing Edward's shoelaces.

"Shouldn't you be in school?"

"It's Saturday."

Edward routinely lost track of days, so that information didn't surprise him. What did make him pause were the silver tear tracks visible on Keegan's cheeks. He remembered all too well being a boy and hiding somewhere to cry in peace. He hastily put two and two together and came up with the reason for the boy's tears.

"Your small cousins, they are still gone?"

Keegan nodded, his shoulders slumped, head hanging.

"Then perhaps your aunt should simply pay the money and be done with it, no?" Edward's voice was harsh. He had no time or patience for the games these wealthy people played. "What is money when children are at risk?"

"He didn't even ask for money," Keegan burst out. "It would be better if he did. My aunt would just pay him and then the twins could come home."

"No money? Then who is this *he* and what does he want with the children? And if the man is known, then why do the police not apprehend him?" By now the entire Massachusetts police force would be up in arms, Edward thought cynically, trying to locate the precious Cooper progeny.

"The police don't know. And if they find out, he said he'd kill Randi and Robin. So don't tell them— please don't say anything, Mr. Gaton."

"So you know who I am?" Edward was surprised. He believed he was anonymous in the village, except to that sullen girl with the wild hair that changed color every week. He could swear she'd been stalking him. Twice he'd caught her following him along this very path, but when he turned to confront her, she was gone. She was a wily one, that girl. She looked vaguely familiar, and yet he was certain he'd never seen her before.

Keegan nodded. "Sure I know. You're the guy who's writing a book. Everyone knows that."

His announcement annoyed Edward. He liked being anonymous. "And you are the son of Clint Cooper, who just married Beth, the pretty librarian," he countered. "Keegan Cooper, is it not?"

Keegan nodded. "My dad's on his honeymoon."

"But he is hurrying back now, no? Because of this kidnapping episode."

That was the thing he'd always envied about having a family. They rallied around you when you needed help. Not that he knew anything about that, Edward reminded himself bitterly. There'd been just him and his grandmother, and now that she was dead, he had no one. Not that she'd been any support in the last years of her life, anyway; she'd regressed to childhood, and he'd had to be parent to her instead of grandson. He'd done it willingly, but it had added fuel to his anger at those who had robbed her of a chance for a decent life. It would have taken so little money on their part.

Keegan shook his head impatiently. "I just *told* you,

we can't let anyone know, not even my dad. If he comes back, the kidnapper will guess that Aunt Maureen told. And then—'' his voice wobbled and he had to swallow hard ''—he'll kill Randi and Robin.... He said so. On the phone.''

Dieu. It was far more serious than Edward had guessed.

In the distance, they both heard someone calling.

"Keegan? Keegan."

"They are looking for you. Answer them, boy.''

But Keegan shook his head.

"I gotta go now.'' He snatched up the puppy and would have bolted if Edward hadn't grasped the back of his jacket and held on.

"Let—me—go.'' Keegan struggled. He was clever enough to try and slip out of the jacket, but Edward had been in far too many street brawls not to know that trick.

"You are running away, is that it, Keegan Cooper?''

The boy was crying, hard, dry sobs. The puppy slipped out of his hands and landed in a heap on the ground. It yelped and then righted itself and squatted to pee, spraying Edward's boots.

"Why are you running?'' Edward couldn't have said why it mattered to him. He should have just let the boy go. It wasn't his concern if this young Cooper bolted. The Coopers were less than nothing to him. But he hung on. "Why are you running away, a boy with everything anyone could want?''

"Because it was my *fault.*'' The profound misery

in the boy's voice touched something buried deep in Edward, and he took hold of Keegan by both arms, turning him so he could look into his face.

"How is it your fault?"

Tears and mucus were mingling on the boy's cheeks. "I was s'posed to be watching them. And I went to the bathroom, and that's when it happened."

"Aaagh." Edward made a deprecating noise in his throat. "That doesn't make it your fault." For the first time in years, he remembered something his *grand-mère* used to say to him when he was little. "When did the good God put you in charge of the universe?"

Keegan swiped at his face with the back of his hand and sniffed, then said in a sullen tone, "I don't know what you mean."

"Think about it, you're a clever lad. And try to realize that running away only makes more trouble for those who care about you." He gave Keegan an impatient little shake. "They are calling you. You are a fortunate boy to have a family who comes looking when you run this way. Now go to them, and try to help instead of causing more problems."

The voices were coming closer. Edward let go, wondering what the boy would do.

When he sank down on his haunches on the leaves again and didn't run, Edward was the one who hurried off, in the opposite direction from the searchers. As he crested the hill and strode down the other side, he had a clear view of the house his ancestors had built and named Twin Oaks.

CHAPTER FIFTEEN

AT TWIN OAKS, THE PHONE RANG.

Maureen's heart began to hammer so hard she wondered if she'd be able to speak.

She lifted the receiver, praying it was Owen.

"He-hello?"

"So, mama. You think you want your brats back today?" The sly, oily voice snaked through the receiver.

"Please." The word came out a whisper. "Oh, yes, please." She cleared her throat and sank into the chair Harry placed behind her. He put a yellow legal pad and a pen down in front of her.

"What do you want?" Her voice was stronger now. "I'll do anything you say—anything. Just please don't hurt them."

"I already told you the rules."

Terror filled Maureen. She was certain he was toying with her, that he knew that almost everyone in Cooper's Corner was aware of the kidnapping. Would he make her pay? Oh, God, would he make her listen while he hurt her beloved babies? Would he—

Her heart was a wild thing, smashing against her ribs.

"Just keep on following the rules and your brats will be okay."

He didn't know. By some miracle, he didn't know.

Maureen sent up a grateful prayer and scribbled as he snapped off instructions.

"Drive to the abandoned quarry south of town, and make it snappy. You make sure you're alone. There's a flat space just north of the quarry. Park your van there and walk away from it. Walk east and keep walking until you hear from me. Anybody comes with you, or you bring weapons of any kind, bitch, and these brats *die,* got that? Little chicken necks like theirs— one snap'll do it."

Nausea and rage and horror almost choked her. "Yes. Yes, I promise, no weapons. I'll come alone, I promise. Then what?"

The evil snicker made her shudder. "Then you wait for orders like a good little girl. You want to see your brats alive, you don't ask questions. You don't tell anybody."

"Let me talk to them. How do I know they're—"

"This is my show, remember? I say what happens, not you. You just do as you're told."

"I will. I'll be there as soon as—" But the connection was already broken. She couldn't get her breath. It took three attempts before she could put the receiver back in the cradle. Her fingers were numb, her entire body shaking as if she had palsy. She knew now what Nevil was planning. He was going to murder her.

She couldn't think of any way to prevent it. But the

twins had to survive. There had to be a way to save them.

Harry put a cup of coffee in front of her. Lydia put an arm around her, patting her back.

"That—that was him," Maureen whispered through lips that felt frozen. Of course they already knew. She tried to move, but her knees wouldn't support her. She grasped the edge of the counter and held on, willing herself to move, to think, to take charge.

"I've got to—to go. I've got to hurry. There isn't much time."

"Wait until Chance gets back," Harry urged. "Or let me come with you."

"*No*. No, I have to go alone. You can't let anybody know. He said if I don't go by myself, the twins will—" She stopped. It had just dawned on her that unless someone else was there, her daughters would die with her.

The only one who would understand what had to be done was Chance. He'd promised to save the twins— he'd given his word. He was the only one she trusted.

Reaching for the pad and pen, she scribbled a note for him, telling him exactly what Nevil had said, where she'd be, what he'd said about being unarmed and alone. At the end, in big block letters, she printed PLEASE COME ALONE, PLEASE KEEP YOUR WORD. She signed it, *I love you, I always have, I always will.*

Now, when it was too late, she knew how true that was.

She folded the note in half and handed it to Harry.

"Make sure Chance gets this the instant he comes back."

"Absolutely." Harry pocketed the note, his brow creased into anxious lines. "But please, let me at least follow you in my car—"

Maureen shook her head, but she wasn't really listening. She had to think, she had to think like a detective, not like a victim. Not like a mother.

Frank had given her a bulletproof vest after Blake Weston was shot. Maureen raced to her room, tearing off her flannel shirt, then buttoning it on again over the protective vest.

In the hall, she snatched the keys to the van from the Peg-Board. Lydia was wringing her hands, her face ashen.

"Be careful, Maureen," she begged. "Please be careful." She gave Maureen a hard hug as she headed out the door.

"Don't tell anyone—promise me you won't tell anyone," Maureen begged in the now-familiar litany. "My babies' lives are at stake."

Standing at the top of the steps holding hands, both of the Joyces promised Maureen she could trust them.

Maureen raced down the stairs and into the van, her mind jumping from one possibility to the next.

There has to be a way to save the twins. Dear God, let me find a way. And if I fail, then let Chance find a way, she prayed as she turned the keys in the ignition and spun the wheels out of the driveway, turning south toward the abandoned quarry, certain of only one thing.

She'd fight for her girls' lives with everything she had. She'd fight Nevil until she no longer had life in her body.

BILLY KEPT THE GIRLS in the bedroom while the fight was going on.

At first, their chins wobbled and they cried as the shouting and cursing from the other room kept getting louder, but after a while they quieted, huddling down with him in the corner behind the bed, holding tight to each other.

Billy and the twins had been sitting at the kitchen table when Owen came. They were all finishing the bowls of cornflakes that Rocky had set out for them. Rocky had been there when they woke up, and he liked the twins. He'd teased them and said they were cute, and even made them smile. Billy wondered why Angie didn't see how much nicer Rocky was than Owen. He also wondered why she'd take a chance like this, having Rocky here when he'd overheard her telling Owen last night to come and get the twins in the morning.

Owen hadn't phoned before he came, and although Rocky was gone already, he'd left his after-shave stuff in the bathroom. When Owen found it, he got real quiet at first, the way he did when he was really mad. Billy hurried the twins into the bedroom, but they'd heard Owen slapping Angie and calling her really bad names. Then she started swearing and crying and hollering back at him. And now they were having this great big fight. The neighbors upstairs had already banged on the floor with something, but it didn't stop them.

"I'm not taking care of your stinkin' brats one more minute," Angie screeched. "You take them, you take Billy, too. For what you pay me, it ain't worth my while to have him around. And you get out of my house, Owen Nevil, and don't ever come back this time. I got somebody who treats me a whole lot better than you ever did. You got no right barging in here this way. You got no ring on my finger, or in my nose, either."

Owen swore at her and then Angie screamed again. There was the sound of dishes breaking and chairs falling over. The twins put their hands over their ears and shut their eyes tight.

Billy got up and grabbed his backpack and started stuffing things inside fast. He knew from past experience that he could get dragged away any minute and then his books and his electronic game and all his things would be left behind.

Sure enough, even before he was finished packing, the bedroom door smashed open, hitting the wall. Owen stood there, his dark face fierce, his eyes red with anger.

The twins shrieked in fright and started to wail. Billy cowered back against the bed.

"Billy, you get your ass out here, and bring those squalling brats with you. Move it," Owen snarled. He took several menacing steps toward the twins, his hand held up. "You two shut up, or you'll get something to cry for."

They went on crying, but they'd learned how to do it without making any sound.

Billy tried to soothe them as he pushed the last of his stuff in his bag and herded the twins down the hall and out the open apartment door. There was no sign of Angie.

Owen banged with his fist on the elevator control panel and swore when it didn't come right away.

The moment the door opened, Billy pulled the twins in before Owen could get mad at them for not moving fast enough.

Billy wondered if he'd ever see Angie again. He didn't much want to. She hadn't been very nice to him, but at least with her he pretty much knew what to expect.

With his brother Owen, he didn't. And what you didn't expect with Owen was always worse than anything you could ever imagine.

TRUDI WASN'T SURE WHAT to expect from Mr. Maguire, and it scared her. She'd made a bad slip back there and he'd caught her at it. She thought of running back to Tubb's, but she knew sooner or later Mr. Maguire would find her there, anyway. There didn't seem much else to do but get the dog the way she'd promised.

Sheba and the two puppies were in the fenced run Jon had made for them at the back of the trailer. It was tricky, getting Sheba out without letting the pups loose, but Trudi finally managed it. She latched the run carefully and patted Sheba, who was whining and nosing at her pups through the chicken wire.

"C'mon, girl. Let's go find Keegan and your other baby." With the dog at her side, Trudi trotted reluctantly back to where Mr. Maguire was waiting.

"By rights we oughta have something for her to smell, so she knows what she's looking for," Trudi explained to him. "But Keegan has Sheba's puppy with him. Maybe she'll track them by the smell of the pup."

Trudi led the way, taking the general route that Keegan had followed when he was running away from her. Sheba didn't pay much attention at first, just bounded around in the underbrush and barked at a rabbit, but just when Trudi didn't know which way to go next, the dog whimpered and seemed to scent the trail. She went running ahead, her nose traveling from one side to the other.

Mr. Maguire stopped every now and again to call Keegan, but there wasn't any answer. They were getting close to the creek, and all of a sudden Sheba began to bark and run faster, scampering along to where the creek had dug a path between the trees.

Keegan and the puppy were waiting there. Keegan was sitting on the grassy bank of the stream, and by the time Trudi got there, Sheba was giving her baby a good going over with her tongue.

"She's Satin's mommy," Trudi explained. Keegan looked dazed, and she didn't want to say anything that would send him running off again. He nodded, and then scrambled to his feet when he saw his uncle, who'd been a few yards behind Trudi and the dog.

"Hello, Keegan. You okay, son?"

Trudi gave him credit. He knew enough not to start in on the kid right away. She'd been anxious about that, afraid Keegan would get a beating for running off. She'd seen enough beatings to last her a lifetime.

Mr. Maguire must be mad at him for making him come looking, but he didn't show it. He just sat down on the bank beside Keegan.

Trudi crouched down by the dogs. Sheba was lying on the dried grass, panting, and the puppy was crawling all over her mother, licking her face and then trying to nurse. Trudi was surprised. She'd have thought Satin might have forgotten that by now, but maybe dogs always remembered their mother. None of them ever knew their father, though. She knew that for certain.

"You came here just to find me, Uncle Chance?" Keegan's voice sounded choked.

"Of course, son. We were worried about you. I met Trudi, and she told me you were feeling pretty bad when she saw you earlier."

Keegan shot Trudi a mutinous look, and then he mumbled something under his breath.

"Sorry, I didn't hear you, son." Chance sounded as if they had all the time in the world. Trudi watched him and Keegan, thinking how different these people were from the folks she'd grown up with. The first thing she'd have gotten for running off was a beating with a belt that would have left her black and blue.

"I said I don't want to go back with you." Keegan's voice was loud now, defiant and belligerent, and Trudi wondered what Mr. Maguire would do about that.

"I won't go back there," Keegan insisted.

"Why's that, Keegan?" His voice was calm and there was no sign at all that Mr. Maguire might be royally pissed off with the kid.

Keegan hung his head and his shoulders slumped. "Because of what happened. Because of what I did."

"Far as I can see, you did everything any boy could possibly do, and you did it perfectly." Mr. Maguire made a list on his fingers.

"You called your aunt right away when you realized the girls were gone. You were the one who found the tool that cut off the lock. You found out from Trevor about the van. You had the sense to call me, for which I'm in your debt."

"But I let them get taken."

"Oh, so you saw it happen. You just stood there and let whoever it was carry off the twins."

Mr. Maguire's words surprised Trudi. She could tell that Keegan was surprised by them as well, and shocked.

"I'd never do such a thing. I'd have fought them if I saw."

"Of course you would. So why did you say you let them get taken?"

"I was s'posed to watch them."

Mr. Maguire nodded. "Tell me, Keegan, have you

ever been around when your aunt Maureen left the
twins alone in the yard for a couple of minutes?''

Keegan thought about it. ''Sure. Everybody has to
go to the bathroom. Sometimes Aunt Maureen leaves
them in the yard on their own.''

''Just as you did.''

Keegan took several moments to think it over. ''I
guess so.''

''It could as easily have happened when she was
with them, Keegan. It just so happened it was you, but
it absolutely isn't your fault.''

Mr. Maguire reached out and put a big hand on
Keegan's shoulder.

''If it's any consolation, I feel every bit as helpless
and responsible as you do. Being a man doesn't mean
you do things right all the time, or even half the time.
In fact, I've made so many mistakes I can't even count
them. You know, Keegan, I didn't even know I was a
father until you called me.''

''Aunt Maureen never told you?''

''She tried several times, but I wouldn't talk to
her.''

''Wow.'' Keegan sounded as surprised as Trudi felt.

''Because of my pigheaded attitude, I've never even
held my own babies. And since I've been here, there
hasn't been a single really concrete thing I've been
able to do to get my girls back. It's just about killing
me, the frustration of it. If I got into blaming myself,
I'd have plenty of ammunition.'' His deep voice was
rough with emotion. ''There's a big difference between blaming yourself and taking responsibility, Kee-

gan. Blame doesn't do a damned thing positive, far as I can see. Sometimes all a guy can do is just be there when the ones you love need you. You help by doing whatever you can, even if it doesn't feel like much. That's responsibility.''

Trudi was listening every bit as attentively as Keegan. Some of the things Mr. Maguire said seemed to shoot straight to her heart, ripping open places she'd tried to close off.

''I guess God doesn't expect us to take care of everything,'' Keegan remarked thoughtfully. ''I guess he has his own plans for things.''

''That's a good way to put it, Keegan. I never thought of it that way before.'' Mr. Maguire sounded surprised and impressed.

Trudi certainly was. She'd never thought about it that way before, either. It sort of took the guilt away.

''I left your aunt waiting for a call from the kidnappers, Keegan.'' Mr. Maguire got to his feet. He had leaves on his backside but he didn't seem to care. ''I don't want to leave her too long on her own. Do you think you could come back with me and help hold things together? Without your dad around, it seems you and I are the men in the family just now, and I sure could use your support.''

Keegan didn't hesitate this time. He nodded. ''Okay. Let's go.''

''I'll take Sheba back to her other puppies, you guys go on ahead.'' Trudi scooped up Satin and handed her to Keegan. ''See ya.''

''Trudi, thank you.'' Mr. Maguire held out his hand

for her to shake. She hesitated a moment, and then hers was engulfed and held in a warm grip. He had really blue eyes that seemed as if he could look right through you.

"If you decide to talk to me, I'd appreciate it," he said in a quiet tone. "You seem like a woman who cares about others. If you know anything, Maureen and I desperately need your help, Trudi."

She nodded. There were some nice men around. She'd thought they were all alike, but Cooper's Corner had taught her she was wrong about that, too. She'd been wrong about so many things.

"You're sure you're okay going back by yourself?" Mr. Maguire gave her a wry look. "Not that I'd be much help with directions. I'm counting on Keegan to find the shortest way."

"I'm fine. I know my way around here."

She did, and as soon as she had Sheba safely in her pen, she followed the path back to the village. But she didn't go straight to Tubb's Café.

Instead, she headed for the public phone booth tucked in beside the gift shop. Her heart was hammering fit to burst, but it was time to take responsibility.

CHAPTER SIXTEEN

TRUDI KNEW THE CELL NUMBER off by heart, and she dug a handful of change from her pockets and dialed it.

It rang four times and she was suddenly terrified he'd just disappeared.

"What?" His voice was as surly as ever, and she could tell that he was in the van by the sound of the motor.

"Owen, please bring them back," she blurted. "You promised you wouldn't hurt them, they're just babies. Bring them back and drop them off outside of town. Tell me where and I'll be there and take them home. I'll take the blame, I promise."

He laughed, that cruel, sneery laugh that made her throat feel dry.

"You're chickenshit, that's what's wrong with you. No guts, but then what can you expect? Your ma had no guts, either. I never understood why the old man ever married her, whiny, sniveling slut that she was. You and Billy boy, both gutless trash, huh, Trudi? Not a brain to share between you."

That's not true. She used to almost believe him when he said things like that, but she knew now he was wrong. She forced herself not to react, not to cry, not to beg him to let her talk to Billy. Was her little brother in the van right now? She strained to listen, but she couldn't hear anything except Owen.

"You know the bargain, Trudi. You're the one who kept tabs on what was going on in that dump of a town." His voice took on the threatening note she was all too familiar with.

"Remember, the cops'll throw you in the slammer same as me if they find out. You're eighteen now, not a juvi anymore, so you better keep your trap shut. You double-cross me and you know what'll happen. Even if you don't go to jail, you'll never see Billy boy again, one way or the other."

"You promised." Her voice was shaking. Her whole body was shaking. "You said if I did this one last thing for you, I could take Billy and go. You promised, Owen."

Over the noise of the motor, she heard stifled little sobs, and then Billy's voice saying something soothing. *He was there. The twins were there, too.*

"He's your little brother, Owen." She tried bravado, even though she was shaking so hard she could barely stand. "You can't hurt him, he's your brother same as he is mine."

"Half brother. Same as he is to you. Hasn't got the makings of a Nevil, either. He got bad blood from your side."

"Then if you hate us so much, why don't you just let us go?" She knew reason never worked on him, but she couldn't help herself. "I can take care of Billy now on my own. Just leave him with the twins and you don't ever have to see any of us again.''

''Sure, sure. When the bitch is dead, then you two can go. When she pays for what she did to Carl, then we'll be even.'' His voice dropped, and he spat out, ''Trouble with you, you got no loyalty to your own family.''

You and Carl aren't my brothers, her mind screamed in silent protest. *You're my stepbrothers. Only Billy is my real brother. He and I had the same mother.* But she couldn't speak, because the certain knowledge that he was planning to kill Ms. Cooper sickened her.

Perspiration soaked her underarms and trickled down her neck, but she felt icy cold. ''You can't— you never said you were going to—you can't hurt the twins, Owen. You said you wouldn't hurt them—''

''And I'm not, right? The brats are fine, sniveling away. I never promised a thing about the Cooper bitch. And since when do *you* tell *me* what to do? Anyhow, it's going down now. By the end of the day it'll all be over and you and Billy boy can split.'' He laughed his evil laugh. ''Maybe.''

She'd blocked off the knowledge that he'd tried many times to kill Ms. Cooper. Trudi had been part of those attempts, telling him what was going on at Twin Oaks and where Ms. Cooper was likely to be at any given time.

It was too horrible to think about, and she'd managed not to.

Until now. Those other times, she'd prayed hard,

and Ms. Cooper always got away okay. But this time was different. This time, Trudi knew, Owen was going to succeed.

"Please, please let me talk to Billy for a minute," she begged.

"No can do. He's busy. He's keeping the brats quiet so I can drive. Don't pull any funny stuff, Trudi. You do, you'll never see Billy again."

He severed the connection.

Shaking and sick, she hung up. Two old men who hung out in front of the gift shop stared at her as she bent double, clutching her stomach and retching. One of them came over.

"You're the gal from Tubb's, ain't ya? Ya need a ride somewheres, dearie? Abel's got his pickup. He'll drive you home. Looks like yer feelin' a bit under the weather."

"I'll—I'll be okay," she managed to choke out. "I don't need a ride, thanks. The fresh air'll do me good."

He gave a doubtful nod and handed her a tissue, and as soon as she was able, she staggered off down the street, aware of concerned glances and kind smiles.

Even for Billy, she couldn't be a traitor any longer. People here in Cooper's Corner had been good to her, treated her better than she'd ever been treated. The Tubbs really cared about her, and she felt the same way about them. She loved them. She'd been afraid to admit it till now, because in her experience love was something that was used against you, a weakness that left you vulnerable.

When the truth came out, the Tubbs wouldn't care about her anymore, but that was the price she had to pay. A sob rose in her throat and nearly choked her.

What had come clear to her when she heard Mr. Maguire talking to Keegan today was that love was good and right. And something she'd never really realized before—love was the same, no matter who felt it.

The way she loved Billy was exactly the same way Ms. Cooper felt about her little girls, the same way Mr. Maguire felt, too. There was something wrong with Owen and Carl, something evil and wicked and unnatural, which fortunately Billy hadn't inherited.

It's going down now, Owen had said. She had to stop it, she had to try to save Ms. Cooper. She had to warn them, tell them all the truth. *Please, oh, please, don't let me be too late,* she prayed.

Breaking into a stumbling jog, Trudi headed for Twin Oaks, running right past the front window of Tubb's Café.

"NOW WHERE IS THAT GIRL GOING?"

Lori Tubb's flushed, good-natured face was troubled as she watched the flustered young girl run past. Lori was standing beside the booth where Edward was sitting. "I certainly hope those poor Coopers aren't having any more trouble," she remarked. "They've got their plate full, you ask me."

Edward didn't comment.

"What would you like, Mr. Gaton?"

"The breakfast special, if you please. Wheat toast, eggs poached instead of fried, if that is possible."

"Sure thing." Lori nodded and filled his cup with coffee. The café was half empty this morning, unusual on a Saturday.

"The village is quiet today."

"Everybody's busy, I guess. Probably getting prepared for winter." Lori bustled off, and Edward sipped his coffee, feeling the usual sense of rejection. So he was not to be trusted, not to be told that the Cooper twins were still missing, and that in all likelihood the entire village was out searching for them. He was an outsider here, as he'd been his entire life. He went over to the stack of old newspapers on a shelf and selected one, so there'd be no reason to make eye contact with anyone or say good-morning.

He flipped open the paper and drank his coffee, grunting a thank-you when Lori set a generous platter of home fries, eggs, sausage and toast before him.

"Can I sit down?"

Edward started, and stared up at the young woman with the hair so red it matched the trees on the hillside outside the café.

Without waiting for an answer, she slid into the other side of the booth. She was wearing something tight and short, and Edward felt annoyed and self-conscious, sensing that the few other customers were watching and wondering why she was singling him out when there were half a dozen empty booths.

In spite of himself, Edward was also curious. What could she want with him? He was much too old and poor to have such a young woman flirt with him, and by the unsmiling, intense look she was giving him, he doubted that picking him up was her intent, anyway.

"You want a menu, Zaire?" Lori materialized beside the booth, refilling Edward's coffee.

"Just coffee, thanks, Lori." When the mug was full, she put three spoons of sugar in it and stirred, then instead of drinking it, she lifted it and used it to warm her hands, as if they were cold.

Edward cut his toast into neat squares, topped one with a mouthful of egg and put it in his mouth. He found it was difficult to chew with her staring at him that way, however. Had no one taught her it was rude to stare?

He swallowed and laid down his fork, frowning at her.

"You have been following me, Zaire Haddock. Why?"

"I wanted to find out about you. I wanted to see what you did, where you went."

"And why should I be of any interest to you?"

She sipped her coffee finally, waiting to answer until she'd had several swallows.

"Because I think you could be my father."

CHAPTER SEVENTEEN

SHE TOSSED THE WORDS OUT like a challenge.

Edward tried not to show the shock and utter horror he was feeling. The girl was quite, quite mad. He laid his fork down carefully on his plate and looked at her.

Who did she remind him of? It kept niggling at him, even as he shook his head and said in a level tone, "I assure you, Ms. Haddock, you are mistaken. Such a thing is absolutely not possible."

"Why not?"

Her simple query unnerved him. She was still staring at him with those eerie gray eyes, like clear water one could see through.

"I would have had to know your mother, for one thing. I know of no one named Haddock...I never have. And for another, I have always taken the most careful precautions." He wondered why he was even explaining such things to her.

"You used condoms, you mean." She snorted. "Now, why did I know you'd say that? They're not a hundred percent, everybody knows that."

He wasn't about to debate the merits of the birth control he used with this—this manic child.

"What has put this ridiculous idea in your head?"

"Don't patronize me, Edward. I'm not a kid and neither am I an idiot." She gave him a look so filled with disdain he was once again taken aback. "My mom died last year. Her maiden name was Marguerite Truman."

"I don't know anyone—"

"Sure you did, Edward. She was from Seattle. She was on an art-appreciation tour. You met her in Paris."

A numbing sense of recognition came over Edward.

He hadn't thought about Marguerite Truman for years. In fact he'd done his best to forget her right after she left Paris, because he knew it was unlikely he'd ever see her again. She'd been a starry-eyed tourist, visiting the city with a girlfriend...Lorna? Lorraine, that was it.

He and his friend Pierre had picked them up at the Louvre. She was an intriguing girl, honest in a way he hadn't encountered before. She'd told him about the boyfriend back in Seattle, and the fact they'd probably marry. She said she'd only ever been with him, and she didn't want to go through her life wondering what it might be like to make love with someone else, so she was experimenting on Edward.

There'd been only that one night—but he'd used protection. Even at a time in his life when hormones raged, he'd always been careful.

He didn't remember exactly what Marguerite looked like, but he knew she didn't in the least resemble the girl across the table.

"My dad's name is Dave Haddock. He's the one who helped me locate you."

"Why would he do such a thing?" Edward was hardly aware of what he was saying. Shock was rippling through him, and a sense of outraged denial. He, of all men, to be accused of fathering a child and not taking responsibility for its care, its future—it was preposterous. It couldn't be so.

"Because I asked him to," she said in a matter-of-fact voice. "My dad will do anything for me. Because I'm his *kid*," she added, as if Edward was the one with mental problems.

"It is not possible," he repeated, more vehemently this time.

"Look, Edward, chill out, okay? I know you're not loaded, and I want you to know right up front that I don't need anything from you like money or stuff, so don't go all wingy on me. My dad has money and my grandmother left me a trust fund. All I want from you is to know what sort of people I come from, who my birth relatives are. I mean, I've got a right to know what sort of genetic makeup I inherited, right?" The gray eyes held his like a vise. "And I need to know if there's any, like, ax murderers or whatever in the family tree."

He could feel manic laughter rising in his chest. It was like a play with a monstrous ironic twist at the end of the second act. He'd thought he was in charge of his life, and now God was laughing at him.

He struggled to make sense out of something, anything she had told him.

"You said your father helped you find me. What do you mean? What about your mother? Why did she not—if this is true, why did Marguerite not contact me, tell me what had happened?"

"Because she loved my dad," Zaire declared simply. "See, she was engaged to him before she came to Paris and met you. When she came home pregnant, they talked it over and decided to just get married quicker than they'd planned. In one way, it was a good thing, because they couldn't have kids, my mom and dad. Of course I didn't know that until just lately either. See, I grew up thinking that my dad was my real father. It was only after my mom died that he told me the truth, and believe me, when I found out, I was some pissed off. The reason he told me at all was because his sister's son, my cousin, was born profoundly deaf. It's apparently an inherited thing in my dad's family, and I flipped out and said I didn't want to have kids because it could happen to me, deaf kids. To my kids. So then he told me that he wasn't genetically linked to me at all, although he'd always be my dad. And then when I got over being really, *really* mad at him and my mom, I got worried about what other things my kids might inherit that could be worse than deafness. So Daddy promised to help me find you."

"And how did he manage that?" His prized illusions about privacy and anonymity were disappearing fast.

"My mom had told him everything about you, so he knew your name and where you were originally from. He hired a detective, but you'd moved around a lot. Then the detective did a trace on you through the police computer and found out you'd been arrested. You gave the cops your employer's name and address, and the detective found out you'd been working in the publishing business. After that it wasn't hard. One of the editors you used to write for said you'd come up here to write a book.''

Edward bristled, furious that his whereabouts were such public knowledge. "And why did you not tell me this as soon as you arrived here? Why did you skulk around, spying on me this whole time?"

"I didn't skulk around," she said in an indignant tone. "I just sort of watched you. I knew you had a record for assaulting a police officer, so I was scared maybe you were some kind of desperate nutcase."

"It happened during a march protesting those soldiers who fought in Vietnam and fathered children there, who were then deserted and forgotten about when the men returned home. Someone threw a stone at one of the protestors. It became a riot, and in the melee I punched an undercover policeman."

She grinned at him. "Way ta go."

This girl and her unpredictable reactions kept throwing him off balance. "I do not regularly go about assaulting policemen," he told her with dignity.

"I know you don't. I've watched you, and apart from being a sourpuss, you're not bad, Edward. See, I wanted to know how you acted on an everyday basis. I watched you feed those squirrels outside your cabin, I saw you carry old Mrs. Goodfellow's groceries home for her. I needed to see what you were like when you figured nobody was watching. I knew once you found out about me, you'd be different.''

She had a point. Edward doubted that anything would ever be the same again, now that he knew about her. His entire world had shifted on its axis, his firm convictions were suddenly shaken, and the bitterness that fueled him now had another side to it. How could he write about servicemen who'd fathered babies and abandoned them, when in front of him was living proof that, in a fashion, he'd done the same thing himself?

As if she'd read his mind, she said, ''So what are you writing your book about? I asked all over town, but nobody seems to know. They're all curious about it.''

He looked at her, at the sharp planes of her face, the line of her cheekbones, the deep-set, clear gray eyes, and he suddenly knew who she reminded him of. She looked like his grandmother, Cecile. Cecile's eyes had been blue, but apart from that, Zaire looked like her. He hadn't seen it at first because he'd only known Cecile as an old woman, but he knew this was how she would have looked when she was young. He had a picture of her somewhere. The recognition took away the last shreds of doubt about who Zaire was.

''The book is about the lost children of war,'' he said. ''It's about the illegitimate children American servicemen fathered all over Europe and then abandoned, knowingly and unknowingly.''

''Did that happen to someone in your family?'' Incredibly, she made no connection to his liaison with her mother and her own birth.

He nodded. "It did, yes. My grandmother, Cecile, fell in love with an American soldier and became pregnant with my mother, Vivien, by him. He died in battle before Vivien was born. Cecile wrote to his family, telling them what had happened, but they never responded. He had a wife and children here, he was a war hero, so they obviously did not want to know that he'd been unfaithful. I have to admit he did not know about my mother because my grandmother never had a chance to tell him before he died. My grandmother's family died in the bombings, and she had no one to look after my mother so she could find a job. Cecile took in laundry, did ironing, anything she could find to earn a meager living. Then in her teens my mother developed tuberculosis, and there was no money for doctors or clinics or cures. There was barely money for food. My mother died when I was born. I had a twin sister, but she died at birth. My mother was only sixteen. Cecile raised me. It was a struggle, every day, just to survive. As soon as I was able, I went to work in a brick factory. Eventually I was able to go to night school."

"What about your father? Didn't you try and find him, see if he could help you out?"

"My mother didn't know who he was."

She frowned. "How could that be? She *must* have known."

"She did not." It was something he was mortally

ashamed of, and he couldn't imagine why he would confess it to this child.

Perhaps because she was his daughter, if what she said was true.

"My mother went with men for money," Edward said. "It was the only work she could do." He watched understanding dawn, waited for revulsion, and saw only compassion on Zaire's mobile features. "So you see, I can be of no help with that portion of your lineage. I do not know myself." He gave a weak smile. "There may well be ax murderers."

"Wow." He could see her digesting it all. "That's heavy duty. That must have been so tough for your mom. God, she was only a kid. And rough for you, too." She thought for a moment. "I can see why you want to write a book about deadbeat dads, all right. No grandfather, no father." Her brow creased in a frown.

"You said your grandfather died in battle during the war. So you know his name and where he was from?"

Edward nodded. "I do, yes. He was from this very town." He took a deep breath and said aloud what he'd only written down till now. "His name was Charles—Charles Cooper. He was the brother of Warren Cooper, who died a few years ago. Charles was married to a woman from this town, and had twin sons, John and Justin. Justin Cooper was the father of Maureen and Clint Cooper, who run Twin Oaks Bed and Breakfast."

"Oh, my god." She stared at him, her mouth agape.

"They're our *cousins*. Edward, those poor little girls that just got kidnapped are our *cousins*."

She grabbed her jacket and slid out of the booth.

"Where are you going?" He wanted to talk to her further. There was so much about her he wanted to know—there was so much he wanted to tell her.

"To Twin Oaks, of course. To see if there's anything I can do to help. They're our family, Edward, for pity's sake." She glared at him and made an exasperated noise in her throat. "I can't believe you could sit here and calmly eat toast, knowing what your own blood relatives are going through."

"But—but they do not know about me." He was filled with confusion. "No one knows."

"Well, they're going to. Keeping secrets is a mistake." She gave him a look that made him feel ashamed of himself, although he still wasn't entirely sure why. "Families stick together at times like these, don't you know that?"

Of course he knew, in theory. He just hadn't ever been part of such a family, and he certainly didn't consider himself part of the Cooper family. They'd made it clear long ago they wanted nothing to do with him. He'd have to explain it to her later. He hesitated, but not for long.

Pulling out his wallet, he left money on the table.

Zaire was already out the door when he caught up with her.

"I will go with you to Twin Oaks," he said.

CHAPTER EIGHTEEN

AT TWIN OAKS, Harry Joyce came running the moment he spotted Chance and Keegan hurrying up the drive. He was in the back garden, pacing back and forth, obviously waiting impatiently for them.

"She's gone," he burst out. "Maureen's gone off by herself to meet that scoundrel, that kidnapper. He phoned and I tried to make her wait or take me with her, but she wouldn't. She said to give you this." He pulled a folded note from his pocket and thrust it at Chance.

Chance felt terror gnaw at his innards. He unfolded the note and quickly read it. His face blanched. "She's gone to some place called the old quarry." His voice was thick with urgency. "Do you know where that is, Keegan?"

"Sure, I'll show you."

"No." Chance shook his head. "No, you can't come. I have to go alone. Just tell me exactly where it is. Harry, I need your car." Dr. Dorn had driven him from the airstrip, and Maureen had the only vehicle.

Harry nodded. "Sure thing, but I'll come with you."

Again, Chance shook his head. "No. Maureen insists I come alone."

It was because of the promise she'd extracted that he'd save the twins if anything happened to her. He had to get there on time to save all of them.

Please, don't let it be too late.

Urgency made his voice harsh. "Keys, Harry?"

Harry dug in his pocket and then swore.

"I left them in my jacket. It's up in my room." He raced like an ungainly stork toward the house, and Chance cursed under his breath at the delay.

"Mr. Maguire? Mr. Maguire, I need to talk to you."

"Not now. I've got to go." Chance's voice was impatient and he shook his head at Trudi Karr as she came sprinting up the drive toward him.

"But…but it's…it's really…really important, Mr. Maguire. It's about the—the twins." She was panting so hard she could barely get the words out.

"Make it fast." Chance wasn't paying attention. He could see Harry catapulting down the stairs with the keys jangling from one fist.

"I'm—I'm Owen and Carl Nevil's half sister. I'm the one who told Owen all about the house and the yard."

Chance froze. He turned and gave Trudi his full attention. It took every ounce of restraint he possessed to keep from grabbing her. He'd never wanted to hit a woman, but at this moment—

Trudi must have seen something in his face, because she gasped, threw up a protective hand and backed up several steps.

"He's gonna kill Ms. Cooper," she blurted. "I just talked to Owen. I don't know where he is or where he's going, but he's going to kill Ms. Cooper. He told me so. He's—he's mean, and he's crazy. He's got the twins in his van, and he's got my little brother Billy with him, and I'm scared, Mr. Maguire."

She wasn't the only one.

"Here's the keys." Harry shoved them at Chance, who grabbed them and broke into a lope, heading for the Joyces' small green sedan.

"You know where they are, don't you?" Trudi was at his elbow as he unlocked the car door. "You've gotta take me with you, Mr. Maguire," she pleaded. "Maybe I can talk to Owen. Maybe it'll give you time to save Ms. Cooper and the babies. He's got a gun— Owen's always got a gun, and Billy's there. Please, please, let me come with you."

Her words made Chance suddenly remember Philo's pistol. He raced back into the house and up the stairs, grabbing the leather jacket, checking to make certain the gun was there. And all the while his mind was frantically going over what Trudi had admitted.

He came to a decision. It was long past time to call for help.

Outside, he grasped Keegan's shoulders and said in an urgent tone, "I want you to call the police right now. Get hold of that state trooper Maureen knows, Scott Hunter. Tell him exactly what's going on, Keegan. Tell him where we are and ask him to come to the quarry as soon as possible. If he questions anything you say, you get Harry to back you up.''

Trudi, her face as white as the rage Chance was trying to hold back, was already sitting in the passenger seat of the car.

''I've gotta come,'' she said when Chance slid behind the wheel. ''You gotta let me try to make up for the things I've done, Mr. Maguire.''

''Do you know the fastest route to the old quarry?'' Chance was steering the car down the circular driveway, past the rows of twin oaks, and he couldn't help but notice the latest additions, the two small oaks Maureen had planted there the moment she arrived, living monuments to his daughters, just as the other, taller trees commemorated older sets of Cooper twins.

If only his girls were allowed to live, to grow strong and tall like the trees that lined this driveway.

''I know a back route, Jon and I hiked up there once,'' Trudi was saying. ''It's an old road, but I think it's okay to drive on with a car, part way anyhow. It takes you up to that meadow by the quarry. It'll be hard to get close without him seeing you, though.''

She hesitated and then blurted out, ''I also met Owen there once when he came to make sure I was—was doing what he wanted. He likes to be high up where nobody could sneak up on him easy. When we get close, we'll have to get out and walk the rest of the way.'' She gave Chance instructions, and the car bumped and bounced along the increasingly rutted trail.

He had to slow down, there was no choice on this

road, and Chance felt as though he was trapped in a nightmare, trying desperately to save his family but caught forever on a road that led nowhere.

"When we get there, you be quiet," Chance cautioned Trudi in a fierce voice. "Don't close the car doors when you get out, don't make any sound at all, or so help me—"

He shot her a cold, threatening look, and her lip trembled.

"You think I want to warn him, don't you? You think that's why I wanted to come, so I could warn him." She shook her head and her brown hair flew around her face in vehement denial.

"I know you've got no reason to trust me, Mr. Maguire." There was a strange dignity to her tone. "But I want you to know I love my little brother more than anything in the world, the same way you love your kids, I guess. Billy's had a rotten life so far. Our mother died when he was just six months old, and there was nobody to take care of him but me. I was nine when Mom died. What did I know about taking care of babies? So then Owen and Carl got custody of both of us, because we were underage and social services didn't have anywhere to send us." There was world-weary bitterness in her voice. "Owen lied and said they'd take care of us. Social services wanted to believe it. What do they want with two more kids and nowhere to put them? And we moved a lot, so they couldn't keep an eye on us, anyway."

She made a sound in her throat, of fear and repulsion. "He's my stepbrother, Owen, he's no real relation to me. Carl, neither." She shook her head, and then her face softened. "But Billy is my real brother. He was always such a good, sweet little boy. We had the same mother, and he's like me, not like them."

Chance glanced over at her, and the fierce, desperate expression on her face softened some of the anger he felt toward her.

"It's just that…Owen made me do things."

She looked into Chance's eyes, the color high on her cheeks, terrible shame evident in her gaze, and the last remnants of anger turned to pity and revulsion as the full meaning of her words became clear to him.

"He said if I didn't, he'd hurt Billy." She swallowed and turned her head away, looking out the side window so Chance couldn't see her face.

"I could have run away," she went on in a flat tone. "He knew that, but he knew I couldn't take Billy. See, I was just a kid. I had no way to get money for food and stuff for both of us, nowhere to go. So I stayed."

Chance maneuvered the car over a particularly bad stretch of road, feeling compassion for her.

"Didn't you ever try to tell the authorities what was going on?"

She shook her head. "He said if I did, he'd hurt Billy bad. I knew he'd do it, 'cause he hurt me all the time." Her voice was matter-of-fact, and that was even more disturbing to Chance.

"And like I said, we moved all the time. I never got to know anybody I could trust. Not till I came here, and by then it was way too late."

Impotent rage swelled in Chance. Owen Nevil was a beast, not a man.

Chance had wondered, during these past hours, if he really had it in him to murder someone, to shoot him in cold blood, and now he knew the answer.

Trudi was pouring her heart out to him. "Owen told me that if I stayed in Cooper's Corner, if I watched Ms. Cooper and told him stuff about her, that he'd let me take Billy and go away. He promised he wouldn't try to find us, and he wouldn't—he wouldn't—bother me anymore. I didn't really believe him, but I was scared, because he kept Billy with him. He's only let me see Billy twice, the whole time I've been in Cooper's Corner. He said if I did this one last thing—" She swallowed. "If I helped him steal the twins, then Billy and I could go. I knew from the first it was an awful thing to do, Mr. Maguire, I knew it was wrong. But he said he only wanted to scare Ms. Cooper, that he'd never hurt the twins, that he'd bring them back. I guess even then I knew he was lying, but I didn't know how to make sure he didn't hurt my brother. I didn't know where he was, or where Billy was, either."

She drew in a shuddering breath and wrapped her arms around her stomach. "Then when you talked to Keegan this morning, I knew I just couldn't do it any longer. I heard what you said about caring about the people you love, about taking responsibility. And I knew that even—" Her voice faltered. "Even if I go to jail and never get to see Billy again, I can't let Owen hurt Ms. Cooper or the twins."

Chance tried not to think that maybe it was already too late for that.

"Turn right here, and then we'll have to stop in those trees over there," Trudi said a moment later pointing ahead to a grove of aspens. "The quarry is just up ahead."

The car bumped to a stop. Chance pulled on his leather jacket and took out the gun. He opened the chamber and put in a loaded clip.

Trudi watched, her brown eyes going from the gun to Chance's face.

"I'm glad you've got a gun," she whispered in a fierce tone.

When they got out, there was the sound of birds, and a whispering of wind through the trees, but that was all. Chance motioned to Trudi, forcing himself to move slowly in the direction she pointed, up a steep embankment to where the hill leveled.

As they got closer, Chance's blood ran cold. He could hear a man's voice, taunting, high pitched, but he couldn't make out the words.

And then he heard Maureen's voice, quiet and assured, responding to something the man had said, and an enormous sense of relief rolled over Chance. She was still alive.

She was so brave. There wasn't a trace of fear in that voice.

But he was afraid, more afraid than he'd ever been, not for himself, but for Reen and his daughters. He marveled at her strength and incredible courage.

Chance made a downward motion and he and Trudi

began to move in a half crouch, sheltering behind the sparse underbrush on the hillside. Obviously, they were approaching the top of the hill.

It was Chance who caught sight of the van first, an old rusted gray Chevy with curtains on the windows. The doors were all closed. He couldn't see in. His heart twisted. Were his children in there? There was no way to tell.

Trudi touched his arm and pointed. By some stroke of luck, Nevil was standing half turned away from them, about a hundred feet from the van. Maureen was six feet away from him. Chance saw the gun in Owen's hand, and now he could hear what was being said.

Icy fear shot through him. His hand tightened on the pistol.

"—brats can watch you die. It'll give them something to remember you by, right, bitch?"

Chance's brain registered the fact that the twins must be in the van. He lifted his hands and held the pistol firmly, sighting along the barrel, pointing it straight at Nevil. He was grateful now that Maureen had taken him to the police range several times and insisted he learn how to shoot. He'd had a natural aptitude for it, but he lowered the gun without firing.

There was no way of telling how accurate Philo's old pistol might be. If Chance shot and missed, Nevil would surely shoot Maureen, and she was at point-blank range.

He assessed the possibilities. There was really only one. He'd have to try to creep up behind Nevil. Maureen would see him, but he'd rely on her quick wits and steely nerves to keep the man's attention focused on her until Chance was close enough to use the gun.

He pressed his mouth close to Trudi's ear.

"Circle around to the back side of the van, where he can't see you. Open the van and grab the kids and run as fast as you can. Hide until you see the police coming." He searched the ground around them, found a boulder and handed it over. "If it's locked, break a window with this."

She nodded, took the boulder, and silently made her way down the hill a short distance. Chance saw her begin to circle around, and he, too, maneuvered until he was almost behind Nevil. He crouched and moved as swiftly and silently as he could toward the woman he loved and the man who was about to kill her.

TALK, COOPER, TALK, HOLD his attention. Get the perp bragging. They all love to brag....

Maureen was drawing on her police training and every ounce of self-control she possessed. She was trying to keep Nevil talking, trying to pump up his ego and delay as long as possible the instant when he squeezed the trigger of the gun he had leveled at her midsection.

She was viscerally aware of her babies, sickeningly grateful that they were at least still alive, locked in the old gray van parked nearby. She'd heard them crying, heard a voice, muffled but soothing, calming them. So at least there was someone else in there with them.

Easing her weight from one foot to the other, she

kept inching toward Nevil in the faint hope that she'd be able to get close enough to anticipate the instant when he pulled the trigger. In spite of the protective vest, it was unlikely she'd come out uninjured if he shot her at point-blank range.

If he aimed for her head or legs, she'd have no chance whatsoever, but at this instant his gun was pointing at her midsection. Thanks to the protective vest, she might just be able to survive long enough to turn his own weapon on him.

She had just gained another two inches, when she suddenly glimpsed Chance. Her heart leaped and then seemed to stop.

He was crouched down behind Nevil, holding a gun out in front of him, moving rapidly across the open meadow. She forced herself not to look at him, and she prayed that the slight movement of her eyes hadn't already betrayed her.

Talk. Hold the perp's attention.

"Exactly how did you pull off that thing with the woodshed, Nevil? I couldn't ever figure that out—"

Chance was now about twenty-five feet away and closing fast.

A loud crash and the sound of glass breaking startled Maureen, but it also startled Nevil. He swung his head toward the van for an instant, just long enough for Maureen to lunge toward him.

Everything seemed to happen at once.

She was aware of Chance hollering at Nevil to drop his gun. She made a frantic grab for Nevil's revolver and missed, and then she thought for a blinding instant that he'd punched her, because she went flying backward, spinning around. She heard the gunshot after she felt the blow, and immediately afterward, a second retort. As she hit the ground, her last conscious thought was that Nevil had killed Chance, and then blackness swirled and swallowed her.

THE BULLET CAME SO CLOSE, Chance felt the vibration as it missed his head by mere inches. He'd seen Maureen go down with Nevil's first shot, and he knew she was either dead or dying.

He roared out his anguish, and a consuming wave of rage and despair took away any fear he might ordinarily have felt. Icy-cold determination gripped him, and he stood up straight, both hands on the butt of the pistol, finger on the trigger, aiming straight at Nevil's gut. He'd kill the bastard now.

Never shoot for the head or the extremities, Reen had instructed him. *Aim for the largest target, the midsection.*

His finger was already squeezing the trigger when another shot rang out, and Nevil's body jerked. An expression of intense surprise suffused his dark features. He was already falling to the ground when Chance's bullet struck him.

Chance didn't remember running toward the spot where Maureen lay in a crumpled heap. He couldn't tell if she was breathing. He was on his knees beside her when Scott Hunter came racing over.

"Call an ambulance, get help quick, that bastard shot her," Chance shouted at him. He slid a frantic hand under Maureen's shirt, trying in vain to find the wound, praying that the bleeding could be staunched until help arrived.

Incredibly, her eyes opened, wide and terrified, and she gave him a desperate look. A sound was coming from her throat, the horrible sound of a person struggling to get air into her lungs. She bucked in his embrace, her hands grasping his forearms, and for what seemed an eternity to Chance, she struggled to breathe.

"Reen, hang on," he begged. "Please, Reen, hang on until the ambulance gets here."

Certain that she was dying, he held her and told her over and over how much he loved her, how much he'd always loved her and always would.

Chance was unaware of the tears streaming down his cheeks, oblivious to the voices of the other state policemen now converging on the scene, blind to everything except the woman he cradled in his arms.

"Reen, Reen, my love, my life. Don't die on me. Don't you dare die on me—"

By some miracle, her breathing was easing. She tried to reach up and swipe at the tears on his cheeks, but she moaned in pain when she moved. Her eyes, however, were filled with wonder. She'd never seen him cry before.

"The—the—vest," she whispered, still struggling for breath. "Frank gave me a protective vest. The bullet—hit—the vest."

She struggled to sit up, and he helped her, scarcely able to believe that she was uninjured.

"The babies—Chance, the twins—are they...?"

Chance turned his head, aware of footsteps and children wailing, and then two sweet small voices screaming, "Mommy... Mommy... Mommy..."

They charged past Chance like small projectiles, throwing themselves on Maureen with such ferocity she once again fell back on the leaves, but this time she was laughing and crying at the same time, trying to cuddle both small bodies, and wincing at the pain in her chest and ribs.

For several blissful moments, Chance couldn't take his eyes off his daughters. Faces and hands dirty, hair wild and unbrushed, their tiny shorts and shirts stained, they were both wailing so loud it made his ears hurt.

They took his breath away. They were simply the most beautiful children he'd ever laid eyes on.

When he could tear his gaze away from them, he noticed Trudi, standing with her arms curled protectively around a slender, fragile-looking little boy. His mop of dark curls was wild and unkempt, and his face and clothing, like those of the twins, could have stood a thorough washing. But there was such adoration in his expression as he gazed worshipfully up into his sister's face that Chance's heart hurt for him.

Trudi appeared both exhausted and scared, her fair skin pale and drawn tight across her prominent cheekbones. She had a scratch on one cheek, and her hands were cut and bleeding. Her lips were trembling and she swallowed hard every few seconds. When she glanced over at the spot where Owen Nevil's body lay, Chance saw her shudder and quickly turn away.

"Thank you, Trudi." Chance went over to her, trying to put some of the overwhelming emotion he felt into the two inadequate words. "Thank you more than I can say for what you did." He took one of her hands and examined the cuts. "We'll get the ambulance men to put something on these."

Maureen was listening.

"Trudi showed me a back way to get to this place," Chance explained. "And then she circled around and smashed the van window with a rock and got the twins and her brother out. She was planning to hide them if—"

What might have happened, what came so close to happening, wasn't something he could bear to think about right now.

"This boy is Trudi's brother?" Maureen was still dazed. Chance could see her trying to sort it all out. "Nevil kidnapped Trudi's brother as well as the twins?"

"Billy's my little brother, Ms. Cooper," Trudi confirmed. She hesitated, and then added in a rush, "Owen was my stepbrother. His father married my mother, and then after Billy was born, she died." Her voice faltered. "It was me, Ms. Cooper, it was me all the time." She hung her head, burying her face in Billy's hair. "I told Owen stuff about you. I caused you so much trouble. See, Owen had Billy, and he said if—if I—if I did what he wanted, he'd let me take Billy and go somewhere far away from him and Carl. But if I didn't—well, I was scared, but that's no excuse." In a small voice, barely discernible, she added, "I'm sorry, Ms. Cooper. I'm so sorry for everything."

Chance could see recognition dawning on Maureen's face. Her eyes went from Billy to Trudi, and for a moment there was justifiable resentment and anger there, but it quickly faded, and Chance saw compassion take its place. Certainly that was what he was feeling for Trudi, and he knew that when Maureen heard the rest of the girl's story, she'd feel nothing but sympathy for her.

Maureen said in a soft voice, "You rescued the twins for us just now. Thank you for doing that, Trudi."

Trudi nodded and tears began to roll down her cheeks. Her trembling hand compulsively caressed her brother's hair. "They're okay, Ms. Cooper. Billy says he took care of them. He got them stuff to eat and took them to the bathroom. He says they're hungry now, though. He is, too."

"We'll all go back to Twin Oaks. There's enough food there to satisfy most of Massachusetts," Chance assured her with a smile.

Trudi shook her head. "I can't go. I have to go with the police, the trooper told me to stay here until they come and get me." Her voice was shaky. "I told Mr. Hunter about—about what I did."

She swallowed hard and cleared her throat. "I know it's a lot to ask, and I've got no right, I realize that, but maybe—do you think—could Billy maybe…" She swallowed and started again, a note of panic in her wobbly voice. "Just until I can call the Tubbs and see if they'll take care of him for me. See, there's nowhere for him to go. He'll have to come along with me to—to—'' Her voice failed her. She gulped and then added, "If social services get involved, they'll put him in a foster home, and that scares me real bad."

"Of course he'll come home with us," Maureen assured her. She was still sitting on the ground, her arms around the twins. "We'll take good care of him. I'm sure Keegan will take him under his wing."

"Can we take Billy home now? We want to have a pomegrand." Randi left Maureen and went over to take Billy's hand. It was obvious she was fond of the boy.

"Have what, honey?" Maureen planted a kiss on Robin's head.

"Pomegrand," Randi repeated. "Billy said we could have one."

"That's right—he did," Robin supplied, nodding her head in agreement.

Maureen still didn't get it. She shot a helpless look at the boy.

"Pomegranate," he explained. "I promised them pomegranates if they didn't cry last night."

Maureen looked doubtful. "I doubt that the store in Cooper's Corner will have any—"

"We'll find pomegranates if I have to fly them in from New York," Chance promised.

The twins had been casting shy glances at him, and they understood that he was promising them what they wanted. They each gave him big, toothy smiles and he winked at them. They ducked their heads and then shot him coy glances from under their long eyelashes.

He'd never been a slave, but he figured he was about to become one willingly.

"Billy will stay with us until you can come and get him," Maureen assured Trudi.

"I don't deserve it. I know that, but thanks. Thank you so much, Ms. Cooper." Trudi sighed and started to cry again, swiping at the tears with the back of one bleeding hand. "I guess I can stand anything as long as I know that Billy's okay."

Scott Hunter had been hovering in the background while Trudi talked to Maureen and Chance. He stepped forward now.

"An ambulance is on its way, Maureen. How you feeling?"

"I'm not going to the medical center." Maureen shook her head, and Chance recognized the stubborn set of her chin. "I don't need an ambulance. I'm going home with my family."

Scott gave her a dubious look. "You better get checked over all the same. You'll be bruised pretty bad from that slug. It's likely it broke a couple of your ribs."

"I'm not going to the hospital. I'll get Dr. Dorn to check me over at home."

Scott gave her an appraising look, then nodded and spoke into a mobile unit he unclasped from his belt.

Another patrolman had joined Scott, and Maureen introduced him.

"Chance, this is Duff Sperling. Duff, this is my—"

She faltered for one instant, and then said in a clear, firm tone, "My daughters' daddy, Chance Maguire."

Chance had plans for him and Maureen that would make such introductions easier, but this wasn't the time to discuss them with her.

When he looked at the expression on Duff Sperling's handsome, ruddy features, Chance instinctively knew that the tall, muscular patrolman had entertained his own dreams about himself and Maureen.

Chance reached out a hand.

"Pleasure to meet you, Duff." Their eyes collided, and in a second's silent interchange, territory was established and battle lines drawn.

"You'll have to come down to the station at some point, Maguire, and fill in a ton of paperwork," Duff said as he let go of Chance's hand. "There'll be an inquiry into the shooting. I believe your firearm was discharged. Would you give it to me now, please?"

Chance had totally forgotten about Philo's gun. He'd dropped it after firing it at Nevil. He went over and picked it up and handed it to the patrolman, butt first. Duff had him drop it into a plastic evidence bag.

"It's just a formality," Scott assured Chance. "It was my bullet that struck him first, but you were right there, backing me up. Appreciate it, Maguire. Right now, why don't you folks go on back to Twin Oaks. Looks like these two little ladies could use a nap."

Randi and Robin were yawning and rubbing their ears, which had turned scarlet. For the first time since Keegan's telephone call, Chance felt like laughing aloud.

If he'd needed any proof that these were his daughters, their scarlet ears were it. Chance's own ears had always had an embarrassing habit of turning vermilion red whenever he was tired. Maureen used to tease him about it. He glanced at her and she shot him a knowing grin, and then set Robin on her feet.

"Let's go home," she said. She tried to get up and a grimace of pain crossed her face. Chance was beside her in an instant. He slid an arm around her shoulders and under her legs and gently lifted her.

"I can walk."

He'd have liked nothing better than to carry her, but she clung to him for only a moment, and then stood on her own.

"The van's just over there." Maureen raised an arm to point and then gasped and winced again. "Chance, you'll have to drive. I left the keys in it."

Scott assured Chance that he'd have one of the policemen return Harry Joyce's car to Twin Oaks.

"You're gonna be bruised from top to bottom, Maureen," Scott cautioned again. "I'm just mighty glad you had that vest on," he added, his voice rough with emotion.

"Me, too," she agreed. "And I'm also glad you came when you did, Scott. Thank you, more than I can say. How did you know to come up here?"

"Keegan called me. He's a fine boy. He gave me clear instructions and told me exactly what had been going on, and why you didn't tell me yourself." There was reproach in his tone. "You should have trusted us, Maureen."

"I couldn't." Maureen had the twins' hands in hers, and she ducked her head to look down at them. "The stakes were too high."

Scott reached out and patted her arm. "I understand. I'm just glad we got here in time. You go on home now. This has been a tough time for you, Maureen, all these past months, but hopefully it's over now, thank God." He turned to Trudi. "You'll have to come with us."

Her face was parched white. She nodded and wrapped her arms around Billy, giving him a long, hard hug, and then, without looking back, she walked off with Scott and Duff and got into the police cruiser.

Chance looked around for the first time. He was surprised to see that there were three state trooper's cars and an ambulance now parked in the clearing. He hadn't been aware of their arrival. He'd been oblivious to everything except his family.

The police had covered Owen Nevil's body with a green sheet, and Chance was relieved. He didn't want the girls to see it. It was enough to know that the man who'd put his family in such jeopardy would never be able to do so again.

The twins were whining now and hanging on Maureen's pant legs, and he knew she wanted to pick them up, but because of her bruising, she couldn't.

He crouched so that his face was at their level.

"Mommy's got a sore tummy, sweethearts, and I know you're tired," he told them. "How about letting me give you a lift over to the car?"

They gave him long, assessing looks, then turned to

each other, and some silent, approving signal passed between them.

He held out his arms, and first one and then the other stepped hesitantly toward him. He lifted them, curling an arm around each of their precious bodies.

"Is Billy coming, too?"

"Yes, Billy's coming, too," Maureen assured them, giving the boy a welcoming smile.

His daughters felt warm and sturdy in Chance's arms. They were his flesh, they bore his genes. He could hardly take it in, the perfection of them. Each put a tiny, trusting arm around his neck, and he could smell them, their sweaty baby smell somehow already familiar and dear to him.

An incredible rush of emotion flowed over and through him. By the grace of God he'd been given an opportunity to turn his life around, to have what he'd always longed for, a family of his own with the woman he loved more than life itself.

Chance strapped the girls into the child seats in the back of the van, Billy beside them. The ride back to Twin Oaks was filled with new revelations about his daughters. Just as Maureen had told him, they finished each other's sentences. They were voluble about the "bad man" who'd made Billy cry, and the "mean old lady" who'd slapped their legs and hollered at Billy.

He and Maureen exchanged glances, wondering how long lasting their frightening experiences would be. Only time would tell.

As he listened to them chatter, Chance began to notice the tiny differences between them, the slight

variance in intonation, the way Randi took charge
when Robin couldn't quite verbalize what she wanted
to convey. They were both vocal about being hungry.

"You must be hungry, too, Billy," Maureen said.
"It won't be long before we're back at Twin Oaks."

Billy responded with a quiet "Yes, ma'am," but he
didn't talk apart from that, and Chance was concerned
about the traumatic effect the events of the day would
have on the boy. He was older than Randi and Robin,
and there was no telling what horrors he'd witnessed
and suffered in his short life. Seeing his brother shot
and killed had to be traumatic for him, regardless of
what Billy's relationship with Owen had been. His
healing would take time.

Chance pulled the van into the long, tree-lined
driveway of Twin Oaks, and both he and Maureen
gasped.

There were cars parked every which way all along
the drive and in front of the house, and a stack of
bicycles was piled by the front door.

"Oh, my gosh. It looks like the entire town is
here," Maureen said. "How do you suppose they
heard?"

"Telepathy," Chance declared.

He found a spot near the top of the drive and got
out, then opened the sliding back door for Billy and
helped Maureen out. The girls were already climbing
down from their car seats, and Chance watched them
scramble out of the van. Just then the front door of
the house flew open and people poured out, led by
Harry and Lydia. They came pounding down the front

steps and along the drive, surrounding Chance and his precious cargo.

Everyone talked at once.

"The girls are back, the girls are back."

"Oh, thank God."

"Look at them, the dear little things—"

"Maureen, what's happened to you? You can hardly walk, dear." That was Phyllis. "Felix," she bellowed over her shoulder. "Felix Dorn, get over here, Maureen's hurt."

"It's just my ribs," Maureen said. Chance had an arm around her, trying to support her without hurting her. The twins had spotted Keegan and gone racing over to greet him.

Chance made the mistake of saying, "She was hit by a bullet, but the vest saved her life—"

"Bullet? Oh, my good gracious, Maureen's been *shot*." Phyllis was almost hysterical. Her voice rose to a shrill screech. "She should be at the hospital. Get her in our car. Philo will drive. Felix, you go along with her—"

"Come on in the house, my dear, and let's have a look at you." Felix Dorn was paying no attention to Phyllis.

"We've got pumpkin soup and egg salad sandwiches, and there's apple pie and lemon tarts and apple fritters—" Lydia and Harry Joyce listed their wares like eager volunteers at a soup kitchen.

"What exactly happened?" Dr. Dorn directed the query at Chance, because Maureen was having all she could do to walk and breathe and smile at the dozens of people attempting to help her and asking questions at the same time.

"She was wearing a protective vest and she got hit by a bullet at point-blank range," Chance explained, his arm around Maureen as she made her slow way up the steps.

"Let's get you into the library where it's quiet and I can have a look at you. And, Chance, I'll take a quick look at the twins as well, just to make sure they're hale and hearty."

"They're really hungry," Chance told the doctor. "If I get them a sandwich, can they eat it while you're examining them?"

"Absolutely. Can't have pretty girls starving on us, can we?"

Lydia had overheard, and in less than two minutes, she produced a plate of sandwiches for the girls, crusts cut off and bread trimmed into dainty shapes. She handed Chance the plate and two glasses of milk for them, as well.

"While I'm examining your womenfolk, it might be wise for you to just let folks know what really happened," Felix said in an undertone to Chance. "Otherwise people's imaginations will run wild and who knows what fantasies they'll come up with."

Chance was reluctant to be parted for even a few moments from Maureen and the twins, but he turned back to the kitchen and attempted to answer the concerned questions Maureen's friends and neighbors fired at him.

He was honest with everyone, telling them exactly

what had happened. They didn't know that Maureen had been a police officer, and he explained why she'd kept that information secret. He was careful to avoid any mention of Trudi Karr's role in the whole episode, except to emphasize that she'd directed him to the quarry and bravely broken into the van and rescued the twins.

Chance felt increasingly sorry for the young woman, and he didn't want to embarrass Billy. The Joyces were stuffing the boy with food, delighted to find someone who was truly hungry.

After a final barrage of questions, people began talking among themselves, and Chance went over to Keegan, who was standing in a corner of the kitchen. He took him over to the table where Billy was sitting. The boy had obviously eaten all he could, and was now regarding the trays of cookies and cakes and sandwiches with a disbelieving look on his thin, dirty face.

"This is Billy Nevil, Keegan," Chance said, making the introductions. "He's going to be staying at Twin Oaks for a while, and he needs a shower and some fresh clothes. Maybe you could find some of yours that would fit?"

Keegan gave the other boy a long, curious look, and Billy eyed him back.

Of course Keegan would have recognized the name Nevil.

Chance watched for an opportunity to take Keegan aside and explain, and the opportunity came while the women were arranging still more food on trays, and the men were questioning Philo about the gun he'd loaned to Chance.

Maureen and the twins were still with Dr. Dorn, and Chance was getting concerned that the old doctor had found something seriously wrong. He'd go and check in a moment, but first it was necessary to talk to Keegan.

Gesturing to him, Chance then led the way out the door and down the steps, into the back yard. It seemed the only place at the moment for privacy; there were people on the deck, and still more seemed to be arriving. Even the reclusive writer was there, and oddly enough he seemed to be with the redheaded woman from the gift shop. They were in a corner of the garden, talking to Phyllis Cooper.

Keegan didn't wait for Chance to explain. "That kid's name is Nevil," he burst out in an accusing voice. "Nevil's the guy who kidnapped the girls, he's the guy who shot at Aunt Maureen. Why is this kid with the same name staying here with us?"

"Because he has nowhere else to go. He's a victim, Keegan, just as innocent a victim as the twins were." Chance explained how Billy had done his best to care for the twins, and then he told Keegan about Trudi and her role in the kidnapping, as well as her reasons for doing what she did.

"She loves her brother, and all she could think of was keeping him from getting hurt. What she did was wrong, and she's sorry for it, but the police had no choice except to arrest her. She was an accessory to the kidnapping."

"Will she go to jail?"

"I don't know. There's a good possibility that she will, which leaves Billy totally alone. The only other relative he seems to have is another half brother, just as evil as Owen was. His name is Carl, and he's in jail for murder and won't be getting out any time soon."

Keegan thought that over and pursed his lips and whistled. "Dad told me about Carl. Man, that kid really has a bummer of a family."

"Yeah, he really does. Which is why your aunt Maureen said he could come and stay here until Trudi's able to care for him. I think Maureen's counting on you to be a good influence, to sort of show Billy how families ought to be."

Keegan thought it over and then nodded. "Well, yeah. Okay, I guess I could do that."

"Good boy." Chance gave Keegan's shoulder a fond squeeze. "Now I have to go and see how your aunt is, and what's become of the twins."

Chance's anxiety mounted when he found the library empty. He headed down the hallway, straight for Maureen's room.

The door to her bedroom was open, and Chance could hear water splashing and children's giggles.

Maureen was sitting on a chair beside the huge old-fashioned tub, which was filled with water and soap bubbles and small naked girls.

Chance's daughters were splashing each other and giggling.

Maureen turned awkwardly toward him, cradling her ribs, and the smile she gave him was radiant.

"They needed a bath in the worst way," she said. "They're experts at getting into the tub by themselves, but I was beginning to wonder how I'd ever help them out."

"I could figure out how to do that."

Chance grinned at her. She hadn't brushed her hair since that morning. Her jeans and flannel shirt were filthy, and she had a leaf in her hair and a scrape on her nose.

She was the most beautiful woman he'd ever laid eyes on.

"What did Felix say about your ribs?"

"They're bruised, but he doesn't think they're broken. And even if they are, there's not a thing that can be done for them except rest and painkillers, according to Felix. He says I should maybe go for an X ray tomorrow, though."

Chance planned to confirm all that by asking Dorn himself. He suspected Maureen was quite capable of minimizing whatever the doctor had said simply because she didn't want to go to the hospital.

"And the girls?"

"Apart from being hungry, they're absolutely fine. Felix looked them over very carefully." She glanced at the twins, who were chattering to each other and not listening to what their mother and father were saying. Maureen lowered her voice all the same.

"There are no visible marks on them." Maureen's voice was passionate. "But I'd like to get my hands on whoever that woman was who slapped them around.''

''I suspect the police will be asking Billy some questions about her.''

''How is he?''

''Pretty full of food at the moment. Not too clean, but that will come.'' Chance explained about leaving Billy in Keegan's care.

''Maybe you'd better get these girls out of the tub before they shrivel up,'' Maureen suggested. ''They really need a good, long nap. They wolfed down almost all those sandwiches, and now they're sleepy.''

Chance looked at the little girls and tried to figure out how to begin. He'd never had any experience with females this small. At a loss, he gave Maureen a helpless look.

She grinned at him and nodded at a towel.

''Just lift them out and dry them off. You'll get the hang of it fairly quickly.''

''What's your name?'' Robin peered up at him, her chestnut hair plastered to her scalp, soap bubbles on her shoulders, immense blue-green eyes fixed on Chance's face.

Everything in him went still for a moment.

''He's your daddy, Robin.'' Maureen's voice was soft. ''His name is Daddy.''

''Where's *my* daddy?'' Randi was outraged, her lower lip protruding.

''He's your daddy, too,'' Maureen told her. ''He's daddy to both of you.''

Their huge eyes focused on him in absolute amazement. Chance smiled and prayed that he measured up to their expectations of what a daddy should look like.

"Keegan's got a daddy," Randi commented in a conversational tone. "Uncle Clint is Keegan's daddy."

"That's right," Maureen agreed. "And now you two have a daddy of your very own, too."

"Great—he can take us for *burgers,*" Randi crowed.

"I can do that." Chance was incredibly relieved that their expectations included something he could do.

"Can we go now?" Robin looked at him expectantly.

"Nope." Maureen's voice was firm. "Now is naptime. And that bath water is getting cold."

Taking a deep breath, Chance reached for a girl.

She was slippery as wet soap. When he set her down she wriggled and giggled and tried to run off, and he was terrified he'd hurt her. She managed to get his trousers and shirt soaked.

Chance, who'd always been quick and adept, had suddenly become clumsy. He lifted the other twin out, wrapped her in another huge fluffy towel, then somehow patted them both dry. They complained vociferously that parts of them were still wet, and he went through the whole performance again. At Maureen's suggestion, he generously dusted them both with a giant powder puff and perfumed bath powder.

Then, sweating with the effort, he heroically faced

the challenge of helping his two naked daughters dress.

"They only need panties and T's," Maureen directed, laughing openly at him. He pretended to glare at her when he managed to get the underpants on backward and all three females went into fits of giggles.

Fifteen minutes later, the sleepy-eyed twins were tucked in their cots, holding hands and hugging favorite stuffed bears with their free arms. Chance bent and kissed each sweet small cheek, and tears welled in his eyes when both of them wrapped their arms around his neck and kissed him back.

"They're asleep already," he whispered to Maureen a few moments later, partially closing the connecting door.

"They've always been good about having naps and going to bed."

Chance could tell that Maureen was beginning to really feel the effect of the bullet's blow now. She'd moved slowly and carefully from the chair in the bathroom to sit down on her bed, and she looked pale and exhausted.

"I think I might lie down for a while myself," she decided, adding in a rueful tone, "if only I could figure out how to get out of these dirty clothes."

"I can help with that, if you'll let me."

She nodded, trusting him.

Chance felt honored.

He knelt and pulled off her socks, warming her bare feet in his hands for a moment. Tender and careful not to hurt her, he unbuttoned her shirt and slid it from her shoulders. The skin on her back and chest, beneath the edge of her bra, was beginning to turn a deep, ugly purple, and Chance felt a remnant of the rage and fear he'd experienced when he saw Nevil shoot her. He would always be glad that the evil man was dead.

"Better take my bra off, too, please, Chance. I can't reach behind to undo the clasp." Her voice was weary.

Chance unfastened the white lacy bra. Her breasts were round and full. He couldn't help himself. He cupped them in each palm, just for a moment, and closed his mouth around the prominent nipples.

During their marriage, Chance had known her body as well as he knew his own, and the sight of her had never failed to arouse him.

It did so now. He struggled with desire as he unfastened her jeans and slid them off her hips. She was wearing the same white cotton bikinis she'd always preferred. Her hips were narrow, and apart from pale stretch marks across her belly, there was little sign that she'd carried twins. There hadn't been time last night to really look at her, to appreciate her body and her beauty.

She knew the effect she was having on him, and he could tell that it pleased her. Maureen had always been honest and open and wickedly uninhibited when it came to lovemaking.

"I want you, too, Chance, so much it hurts," she said with a rueful grin. "But just at this moment, my ribs hurt even worse. You'll have to take a rain check." There was mischief in her voice when she added, "Just until tonight, though, when those pain-killers Felix gave me have a chance to kick in."

"Can I have that in writing?" He pulled the duvet back and grinned at her as he eased her against the pillows and covered her up.

"My word is my bond." She'd closed her eyes and now she opened them again and scowled up at him. "Unlike someone else I know. I thought you promised me—"

He stifled the rest of it with a kiss that was also a promise, and took her long-fingered hand in his, holding it palm to palm, lifeline to lifeline.

"All's well that ends well."

"That's exactly what Lori Tubb said to me. She knows every aphorism in the entire English language." She giggled and then sighed, the deep, contented sigh of someone at peace with the world. "Thank you, Chance." Her voice dropped to a whisper and her eyes closed. "I love you."

How many times today was he going to have to struggle against making an utter fool of himself by crying?

"I love you, too, more than I can ever say. But I intend to show you, every day from now until forever." He kissed her, just a promise of a kiss, and then sat beside her, holding her hand, until her breathing slowed and she began to snore gently.

He'd never told her that she snored. He figured he never would. It was one of those small, secret things, his alone to treasure.

He tiptoed into the twins' room, just to feast his

eyes on his family, sound asleep and safe. In his care, and in his heart, for the rest of his life. He mustn't forget to have a case of pomegranates flown in from New York, so they'd be here when his girls woke up. He wanted them to know that their daddy always kept his promises.

When he heard his daughters' both snoring vigorously, just like their mother, he had to stifle his laughter. Suddenly he was filled with overwhelming joy, and he was also ravenously hungry.

Harry and Lydia Joyce were going to be ecstatic when they found out just how much food he could consume when he was happy.

EPILOGUE

By 5:00 P.M. ON CHRISTMAS EVE, the snow was two feet deep and still falling. Cooper's Corner was having the white Christmas everyone had given up hoping for. The fall had been unseasonably warm, and when it ought to have snowed in late November and all through the early part of December, it rained instead. At seventy-three, Mrs. Vine swore it was the most peculiar year weather-wise that she'd ever witnessed, although Burt Tubb claimed Abigail Vine said the same thing every year about the weather.

Maureen peered out the window of the blue room. She'd decided to dress in one of the guest rooms upstairs for greater privacy. Cupping her hands, she peered down at the driveway through the swirling flakes. It was crowded with vehicles.

"Is everyone here? Is Chance ready?" She was downright nervous. Had she been this nervous the first time she married him?

"You'd need a shoehorn to fit another person into that living room downstairs," Beth assured her. "And Chance has been wearing a hole in the library carpet for half an hour already." Beth's violet eyes softened as she gazed at her sister-in-law. "You look stunning, Maureen. That amber shade is perfect on you."

"You don't think the velvet is a little over the top?" Maureen glanced nervously into the mirror. "For someone who lives in denim, this stuff is a real stretch."

"It's great." Beth gave her a careful hug, and Maureen returned it with fervor. "You're radiant and gorgeous and everything a bride should be on her wedding day. Clint and I are so happy for you."

Maureen had made the dress herself, recognizing that the sumptuous fabric needed pure, simple lines. She'd made slipcovers and bedspreads and curtains, but this wedding dress was her first attempt at sewing clothing for herself.

The result pleased her. The long-sleeved elongated sheath fit her perfectly, skimming over her body, the hem brushing the tops of the classic satin pumps Zaire Haddock had insisted she have dyed to match. And at her throat and in her ears were the antique pearl-and-diamond pendant and drop earrings Chance had given her just hours ago.

"My family weren't the sort to have heirlooms," he'd told her, "but with daughters, it's never too late to start a tradition. These can be the beginning of the Maguire family collection."

The Maguire family.

She and Chance still had disagreements. Truth be told, they'd had several out-and-out fights in the last couple of months. After one, the twins had scowled at them and ordered, "You two better sort this out."

Ashamed of themselves, they had. They were opinionated, stubborn, independent individuals, and their life together would never be placid.

But neither would it be insecure. There was a permanence about their relationship now, a sense of themselves as a solid unit that would withstand the odd battle, because they were a family. Chance still had to fly to New York several days a week to tend to his business, but he was slowly setting everything up so that he could run it, via computer and telephone, from Cooper's Corner. He felt, as she did, that the village was the ideal place to raise their daughters, surrounded by family, supported by friends and neighbors.

Living in Cooper's Corner had taught Maureen so much about families. Her newfound cousin, Zaire Haddock, had quoted something her own birth father, Edward Gaton, said, and it stuck in Maureen's head.

"When you've got a family, you don't always appreciate them. But if you've grown up without one, you search constantly for your place in the world."

Zaire was an intriguing young woman, and in spite of the age difference, she and Maureen had become friends. She'd told Maureen the story of how she'd tracked Edward down. He was still working on his book, although he admitted it had changed drastically from his original concept. He now was certain that the Coopers had never received the letter his grandmother had written to them. They simply weren't the type of people who would have ignored such a desperate plea for help.

Maureen made a point of asking him to Twin Oaks for dinner at least once a week. He was, after all, another of her cousins. All the Coopers had taken him under their widespread wings, and he smiled a lot more than he ever had.

Unpredictable Zaire had made up her mind she wanted to be on the New York police force, and she viewed Maureen as both a model and a mentor. She also adored the twins, treating them like the baby sisters she'd always wanted and never had.

She'd arrived at Twin Oaks early that afternoon, determined to bathe and dress Randi and Robin for the wedding. The door to the adjoining room flew open now, and Zaire stuck her head out and pretended to blow on a make-believe trumpet. Her wild hair was blue-black this month.

"Make way for the royal princesses," she caroled.

Randi and Robin walked out hand in hand, and Maureen's heart caught in her throat. They actually looked like princesses.

She'd made their dresses, as well, in a deep, rich chocolate brown. Zaire had drawn their chestnut curls up on top of their heads, threading in ribbon that matched the dresses. The dark color made the little girls' fair skin translucent, and their huge eyes glowed like beacons.

"We're gonna marry Daddy, and *then*—" Robin announced.

"Santa Claus is gonna come," Randi crowed.

The three women laughed, but Maureen noticed her eyes weren't the only ones that glimmered with tears. "We'd better get started, then," she said in a deceptively calm tone. "Does anyone have to go to the bathroom?'' There were negative shakes of two small heads.

"Give me five minutes to alert the groom and get to the piano,'' Beth said, hurrying away.

When the hauntingly sweet strains of "Only You'' came floating up the stairs, Maureen took a deep breath and gave the tiny hands clasped in hers a little squeeze, not so much to give Randi and Robin encouragement as to receive it.

"Here we go, my darlings. Everybody smile.''

Slowly, the three of them made their way down the steps, and people in the hallway below grew quiet, marking their progress with tremulous smiles and not a few wet eyes. Twin Oaks had hosted many weddings over the past year, but Maureen knew there had never been as many people present as there were now. The former farmhouse was bursting at the seams, and even more people would be arriving afterward for the lavish buffet dinner Harry and Lydia Joyce had prepared.

They'd asked if Maureen and Chance would mind if they came and prepared the food, as a special wedding gift. Who in their right mind would turn down a gift like that?

Clint met Maureen and her daughters at the bottom of the stairs, and gallantly escorted by him, they made their way along the crowded hallway and then in through the wide doors of the gigantic living room, which was redolent with the smell of pine and roses. Just as Beth had said, it was packed with dear, familiar faces.

One face in particular stood out, and Maureen gave Trudi Karr a special, welcoming smile.

TRUDI WAS STANDING JUST inside the living room, Lori Tubb on one side of her and Burt on the other. Her eyes filled with tears when Maureen acknowledged her. She could hardly believe she was here as an invited guest, in this beautiful room, about to witness this wedding.

It had been two weeks since Trudi had returned to Cooper's Corner. After hearing her story, the judge had been lenient with her. She'd given Trudi an eight-week sentence at a women's detention center, and then released her into the custody of the Tubbs.

Burt and Lori's support had influenced the judge, Trudi knew. The Tubbs had stood by her throughout the hearing, the sentencing, the time she'd spent in jail. They'd been there to pick her up the day she was released, and they'd given her the waitressing job again at Tubb's Café. They were like grandparents to Billy, and Trudi loved them with all her heart.

This morning, Lori had handed her the letter that even now was tucked in the pocket of her new blue dress.

Jon Durham had written her, care of the Tubbs. It was a long letter, but already there were whole paragraphs that she knew off by heart. There was also a return address, in care of a lawyer, where she could write back to him.

He'd left Cooper's Corner the week after Trudi was arrested, so he knew of her role in the kidnapping, her relationship to Owen Nevil. He also knew, he wrote, that she'd gone with Chance Maguire up to the quarry that day. At first he'd been mad because she hadn't confided in him. But then he'd got to thinking about how much courage it must have taken for her to confess her part in the kidnapping.

And after a while, thinking about what she'd done and faced up to had made him ashamed of running away. So he'd gone to the police and told them about his part in the break-and-enter charges, the petty theft he'd been involved in with the gang in New York. He'd given them the names of the gang members who were after him and they'd been arrested. There'd be a hearing, and Jon had no idea what the outcome would be. He had a court-appointed lawyer who figured he'd get off, but he didn't know that for sure. He'd done his share of stealing, just like the others had, and he was prepared to serve a sentence, if it came to that.

What he did know—and this was the part that Trudi knew off by heart—was that he was coming back to Cooper's Corner as soon as he was free. He wanted to see her again. He wanted them to get to know each other without the baggage they'd each been carrying before.

See, Trudi, he wrote, *I have these good feelings about you and me. I figure we both learned the hard way. I know it's a lot to ask, but wait for me, okay? Maybe we can go traveling together. Sheba's fine. She's staying with a friend. She misses you, like I do.* He'd signed it, *With my love, Jon.* Trudi had already figured out what she'd write back. She'd tell him about

Billy. That might make a difference, but she didn't think so. A man who loved dogs as much as Jon did could get to love a boy. She'd tell him that Seth Castleman, the carpenter Jon had worked for, had agreed to take her on as a helper in the spring. Then if she was any good, she'd have to go to school for a while to get qualified.

But she'd also tell him that traveling wasn't an option. Jon had to understand that she was planning on putting down roots in this town, as much for Billy's sake as her own. Billy was going to the village school, and he was doing well. His teacher, Gina Monroe, who was standing with her husband just across the room, had told Trudi that Billy was an exceptional student.

Trudi was determined that Billy would have a chance at a good education, and to do that, he needed to stay in one place. He needed the help that family could provide. She was Billy's family, and so were the Tubbs and Dr. Dorn and his wife.

And so, too, were Maureen and Chance, Clint and Beth, and particularly Keegan. While she'd been in prison, they'd taken care of Billy like he was their own. If it took a lifetime, she'd find a way to repay them all, even though Lori Tubb said it wasn't necessary.

"You only get back what you give away," she insisted. "And love is the best thing to give."

AT THIS MOMENT MAUREEN WOULD have totally agreed with Lori. The gigantic gathering room seemed to vibrate with love and good wishes. It was filled to capacity with the friends and neighbors who'd supported her when the twins were kidnapped.

Those terrible days were far from her mind now as she and the twins, escorted by Clint, slowly made their way across the room.

In front of the blazing hearth stood Chance and Tom Christen, the pastor, but Maureen saw only Chance.

He was so handsome in his perfectly tailored tuxedo that he took her breath away. Their eyes met, and Maureen felt elated and humbled. There was awe in his midnight-blue eyes when he looked at her, and she knew he found her beautiful.

"Hi, Daddy," the twins chorused in unison. They were daddy's girls.

"Hi, my sweethearts." There was a catch in his voice as he bent to kiss them.

The room grew hushed and still.

"Dearly beloved," Tom began. "We are gathered here in the presence of friends and loved ones—"

There was a frantic scrambling and yapping as Satin, the half-grown puppy, came charging through the crowd. Keegan and Billy had been holding her, but somehow she'd managed to break free. She knew her place was with Randi and Robin, and she skidded to a halt and gave each of them a thorough, wet greeting, whining and barking a noisy welcome, her entire hind end wagging with the ferocity of her joy. And then she squatted and made a puddle.

The twins giggled so hard they collapsed to the rug in swirls of brown satin. Maureen was laughing helplessly, and so were all the guests.

It took a few moments for Chance to sort things out. He told Satin to sit and stay, and for the first time in her contrary life, the dog actually obeyed.

He hauled his giggling daughters to their feet and brushed them off as Tom waited patiently.

"Dearly beloved," he began again. "Now that we are *all* gathered here in the presence of friends and loved ones..."

A shiver went trickling down Maureen's spine, and it seemed to her in that moment that Tom was absolutely right. They were all gathered here.

The room was filled not only with those who were living, but also with the benevolent ghosts of Coopers past, her great uncle Warren Cooper and her grandfather Charles, and all the others silently represented by the twin oaks that lined the driveway.

They'd lived and loved, they'd known heartbreak and joy. They were her ancestors, her heritage. They were her link with eternity, just as Chance and her daughters were her connection to the future. They were her family.

"To love, and to cherish..."

Forever.

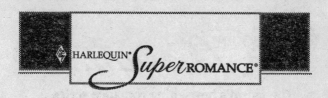

...there's more to the story!

Superromance.
A *big* satisfying read about unforgettable characters. Each month we offer *six* very different stories that range from family drama to adventure and mystery, from highly emotional stories to romantic comedies—and much more! Stories about people you'll believe in and care about. Stories too compelling to put down....

Our authors are among today's *best* romance writers. You'll find familiar names and talented newcomers. Many of them are award winners— and you'll see why!

If you want the biggest and best in romance fiction, you'll get it from Superromance!

Emotional, Exciting, Unexpected...

HARLEQUIN®
INTRIGUE

WE'LL LEAVE YOU BREATHLESS!

If you've been looking for thrilling tales of
contemporary passion and sensuous love stories
with taut, edge-of-the-seat suspense—then
you'll love Harlequin Intrigue!

Every month, you'll meet four new heroes
who are guaranteed to make your spine tingle
and your pulse pound. With them you'll enter
into the exciting world of Harlequin Intrigue—
where your life is on the line
and so is your heart!

THAT'S INTRIGUE—
ROMANTIC SUSPENSE
AT ITS BEST!

HARLEQUIN®

Makes any time special ®

Harlequin® Historical

From rugged lawmen and
valiant knights to defiant heiresses
and spirited frontierswomen,
Harlequin Historicals will
capture your imagination with
their dramatic scope, passion
and adventure.

Harlequin Historicals...
they're too good to miss!